'**Leopard's Claw** grips you from the first line. The adventure in this book is really full-on. I couldn't put it down.'
Lily, age 11

'A unique experience. There's no other book like it!'
Edmund, age 12

'I was scared and excited at the same time. The most exciting book in ages!'
Eleanor, age 9

It arrived on Wednesday just after school. I was so excited. I tore open the package and there it was—**Leopard's Claw**! I set to reading it straight away, not even stopping for tea. By the time I was finished it was time for bed.
Carys, age 11

'A very exciting book! The mystery kept you hanging on . . .'
Tom, age 12

'This book is full of mad, funny, interesting, crazy, sad, scary but cool things . . . Everyone should stop reading what they are reading and start reading David Miller's books.'
Molly, age 12

'Amazing and brilliant.'
Imogen, age 10

'I couldn't bear the suspense!'
John, age 12

Other books by David Miller

Leopard's Claw

DAVID MILLER

OXFORD
UNIVERSITY PRESS

This is for The Norfolk Squad: Alice, Amy,
Charlotte, Daisy and Lucy with love

OXFORD
UNIVERSITY PRESS

Great Clarendon Street, Oxford OX2 6DP
Oxford University Press is a department of the University of Oxford.
It furthers the University's objective of excellence in research, scholarship,
and education by publishing worldwide in

Oxford   New York

Auckland   Cape Town   Dar es Salaam   Hong Kong   Karachi
Kuala Lumpur   Madrid   Melbourne   Mexico City   Nairobi
New Delhi   Shanghai   Taipei   Toronto

With offices in

Argentina   Austria   Brazil   Chile   Czech Republic   France   Greece
Guatemala   Hungary   Italy   Japan   Poland   Portugal   Singapore
South Korea   Switzerland   Thailand   Turkey   Ukraine   Vietnam

Oxford is a registered trade mark of Oxford University Press
in the UK and in certain other countries

British Library Cataloguing in Publication Data

Data available

ISBN: 978-0-19-275612-1

1 3 5 7 9 10 8 6 4 2

Printed in Great Britain

Paper used in the production of this book is a natural,
recyclable product made from wood grown in sustainable forests.
The manufacturing process conforms to the environmental
regulations of the country of origin.

Acknowledgements

To research Leopard's Claw my wife Su'en and I made a six week trip up the Kayan River into central Borneo. We would like to thank the many people who helped make the expedition such a success. In particular, the incredible Mr Fixit—Lucas Zwaal, and Ahmat our guide; our porters Thomas, Asan and Marcos; Chief Anye, Pak Jalung, Andres and all the people in the Kenyah villages of Long Alango, Long Kemuat and Long Bia; and of course the shy but charming Punan tribespeople who taught us so much about their unique way of life.

I also owe a special thank you to Ian Mackenzie for the use of his wonderful Punan dictionary.

Contents

1

Rough Justice

'Nicholas James Bailey, you have been found guilty of first degree murder. You will be executed by firing squad four weeks from this date, at a location yet to be decided . . . '

Dad flinched, as if every badly-pronounced word the judge read out was a bullet slamming into his body. His knees began to buckle. Only the prison guards holding on to him stopped him from collapsing entirely.

For a moment there was silence. Then the crowd in Court One of the Sangabera Justice Building erupted. People who, seconds earlier, had been sitting quietly, leapt to their feet as if under orders, and began to shout, waving their arms in the air. For an instant, Mum was lost in the crush. But then the children saw her launch herself from her seat and throw herself at the judge. *'You can't do this!'* she screamed. *'You've got no proof! He's innocent!'*

A court official tried to stop her, but she shoved him aside. Mum—quiet, kind, *sensible* Mum—had turned into a ferocious beast. She reached the judges' table and climbed onto it, lashing out at anybody who tried to restrain her. She grabbed the judge by the collar of his scarlet and black robe, thrust her face close to his. *'Take back what you just said!'* she yelled. *'Take it back! You know he's innocent. This isn't justice!'*

Panic-stricken, Hanna, Ned, and Jik tried to get to her—but there were too many people in the way. Alarm bells shrilled. Armed police, batons raised, burst into the courtroom. Mum was grabbed by the neck. Other policemen seized Dad, thrusting his arms hard up behind his back, making him shout out in agony. The judge and his two assistants picked up their papers and scurried out of a side exit. 'That's my mum!' Ned was screaming, wrestling with anybody in his way as he fought to reach her. 'Take your hands off my mum!'

Hanna was fighting too. She managed to get to Dad, and hold on to him. For a split second their eyes met. He was saying something to her, she realized—repeating the same two words over and over again. But what were they? It was impossible to tell with all the shouting and screaming. She tried to get him to speak louder, but a baton descended painfully on her arm and her grip was broken. She watched helplessly as he was dragged out of the court and thrust into a waiting police van. Mum was carried out after him and thrown kicking into a second van. Sirens howling, the vehicles accelerated away.

The crowd was growing by the minute as more and more people arrived, attracted by the noise. With Mum and Dad gone, their attention turned to the children. *'Anak kriminal!'* they were screaming. *'Anak kriminal!'*

Hanna knew enough Indonesian to understand what they were saying. They were accusing the three of them of being criminals—child criminals. Punches were thrown. Jik, the Sea Gypsy boy, let out a yelp of pain as a fist caught him in the mouth, making the blood flow. *'We go!'* he yelled at Hanna and Ned, fighting to get away. *'We go now!'*

Fresh police charged into the courtroom, batons flailing. A gap opened up behind them. Seizing their chance, the children dashed for the door.

They reached it, and were through. Three men had spotted them, and were giving chase. Dodging flowerpots and benches, Hanna, Ned, and Jik sprinted through the open doors of the court building and out into the sunlit street of the East Borneo capital. One of their pursuers soon gave up—but the other two were young and fit. *'Anak kriminal!'* they were screaming, their faces distorted with hatred. They were catching up fast.

3

There was a *warung*—a small eating-house—opposite. Jik, who was in the lead, dodged into it. Hanna and Ned followed him. The diners looked up from their food in surprise, as the three children dashed through, scattering chairs, heading for the kitchen. The owner, a thin man with bad teeth, was stir-frying something in a wok. He shouted angrily as they barged past him and into the alley behind the shop.

Their pursuers were close behind, but they were large men, and the kitchen was tiny. There was a cry of pain. One of them had collided with the wok and had splashed himself with hot cooking oil. His companion stopped to help him.

Seizing their chance to escape, the children raced along the alley at high speed. Up ahead was a main road. If they could reach it in time, they could maybe disappear into the crowd and get away.

But there were police sirens, growing louder by the second. They seemed to be coming from all directions at once.

On one side of the alley was a deep storm drain. It was half-full of water and floating garbage. It ran underneath the main road in a tunnel and came out on the other side. Jik pointed at it. 'We go in there!' he yelled.

Hanna opened her mouth to protest, but she

was too late. The Sea Gypsy boy had already leapt into the drain. The slimy black water came up to his knees. He disappeared from sight underneath the road.

Ned was next.

Holding her nose, Hanna followed.

She was just in time. A powerful police motorcycle had turned into the alleyway and was speeding towards them. Praying that they hadn't been spotted, she waded quickly towards the boys.

They waited in the gloom, holding their breaths. The motorbike roared to a halt above their heads. A police car, its siren wailing, drew up next to it. They heard voices. 'What are they saying?' Hanna asked Jik.

'They're asking if anybody has seen the criminals.'

'We're not criminals!' Ned protested loudly.

'Quiet!' Jik ordered. 'Or they goddam hear you!'

More cars pulled up. It was as if the entire Sangabera police force had decided to hold a rally right above their heads. Surely somebody must think of looking into the drain beneath their wheels?

Nobody did. After a few minutes, doors slammed, engines started up, and the vehicles roared off.

Silence fell. Trembling with shock, Hanna peered around her. Floating nearby was what looked like an old sack.

It wasn't.

It was a dog. It had obviously been dead for a long time. Most of its fur was missing, and its swollen belly was split open like an over-stuffed cushion. Where its intestines had once been was a writhing mass of maggots.

'We've got to get out of here,' she gasped. 'We'll catch a disease.'

She turned to go, but Jik grabbed her. 'Wait,' he hissed. 'Maybe there is still a policeman up there. Maybe they play a dam trick to make us think they have all gone.'

'But this is horrible!' Ned protested.

'Better than go to goddam jail!'

They forced themselves to stand still and wait. There was a gentle current and, to Hanna's horror, the dead dog began to drift towards her. She felt it bump softly—slimily—against her bare legs.

She tried to push it away, but it came back again. And again.

'I don't care if there are policemen up there!' she exclaimed, unable to stand any more. 'I'm not staying here a moment longer!'

Her words were drowned by a violent clap of thunder.

A tropical storm, which had been building all morning, was breaking above their heads. As lightning flashed, torrential rain began to cascade from the sky, drumming on the hard surface of the road, sluicing into the culverts.

Within seconds the water level inside the drain had risen to chest height. They had to get out of their hiding place fast!

Half walking, half swimming, terrified of slipping and being swept away, the children staggered towards the light. They were just in time. As the water hit the top of the tunnel, filling it completely, they pulled themselves clear, and lay gasping on the concrete surround. The dead dog shot past after them, shedding maggots like passengers from a sinking ship. It surged away down the drain and out of sight.

They stayed where they were for long time, not moving, letting the rain wash the filth from their bodies. There were all sorts of diseases you could catch from dirty water, Hanna knew—typhoid, cholera. She prayed that nobody had swallowed any.

The storm ended as quickly as it had begun, and the sun came out again. The three children pulled themselves slowly to their feet, not knowing what to do next. As they did so, a voice made them freeze.

'Like drowned rats,' it said in English. 'Like three drowned rats!'

They spun on their heels. A man was squatting in a nearby doorway. He was young—in his late twenties it looked like—wearing jeans and a faded black T-shirt. His hair was scraped into a tight ponytail. He grinned at them, then glanced downwards into his lap.

He was cradling a long-barrelled handgun.

2

Surprise Visit

It had begun with a call from London. Dad, who was sorting out bundles of thatching straw in the barn, took it on his mobile. When he came into the cottage his eyes were sparkling. 'Felix is in England,' he announced. 'He's just flown in and wants to come and see us. I said we'd put him up for a few days.'

Hanna, Ned, and Jik, who'd just arrived home from school and were reluctantly taking out their homework books, glanced up with interest. Was this the same Felix Dad had so often told them about? The German friend who'd travelled the length and breadth of Asia with him during his hippy days? Who'd been to places that no other European had ever set foot in, and lived to tell the tale? Who'd first told Dad about Kaitan—Shark Island—where the children had rescued Mum and Dad after a terrifying pirate attack.

It had to be!

'When's he coming, Dad?' Ned asked excitedly.

'Tomorrow afternoon. I'm meeting him at the station.'

Ned twisted towards his mother who was making a cup of tea. 'That's brilliant, isn't it, Mum?'

One glance at Mum's face told him she didn't think it was. She frowned, stirred her tea loudly, looked up at her husband. 'What's he want?' she asked suspiciously.

Dad shrugged. 'Nothing, as far as I know. It's just a holiday, I guess.'

'A holiday! His whole life's one long holiday! There has to be some other reason for him to come all this way.'

Dad let out an irritable sigh. 'Well if there is, I don't know it. The least we can do is make him welcome, Lin. Besides, he can speak Sama. It'll be nice for Jik to chat to somebody in his own language for once.'

Mum looked across at Jik, and her expression changed. 'Yes, it would,' she said fondly. 'He's doing so well with his English, but it's not the same as speaking in your own mother tongue.'

'Too dam right!' Jik agreed.

'Jik!' Ned warned.

He gave a wry grin. 'Sorry!'

Since he'd come to school in England, Jik had learned fast. He'd almost caught up with the rest of the children in Ned's class, and it looked as if he'd soon be overtaking them. But there was one big problem: Mr Biggs, his teacher, had banned him entirely from using the word 'dam'.

And Jik was finding it *dam* difficult!

The next day was Saturday, and the three children went with Dad to meet Felix at the station. Even though they'd never seen him before, it was impossible to mistake him when he jumped down from the train. He was *enormous*—at least a head taller than Dad—with a deep tropical tan and hands the size of dinner plates. He gripped Dad in a massive bear hug, then turned to the children. 'You must be Hanna,' he roared. 'I can't believe you're only thirteen—you look so grown up! And you're young Ned!' He hugged them both. 'Your dad's told me so much about you!'

To Hanna's surprise, he didn't hug Jik, but put his right hand over his heart in the traditional Sea Gypsy greeting. *'Man-agina!'* he said. 'Greetings!'

'Man-agina!' Jik replied, hugely delighted.

He had gifts, which he handed out when they got home: a bottle of duty-free Scotch for Dad; necklaces made from Burmese jade for Mum and Hanna; and for the boys a *keringon*—a Punan nose flute from central Borneo, which he demonstrated how to play, much to everybody's amusement. The children liked him a lot.

That night Mum cooked a delicious Malaysian curry. After they'd eaten, they sat round the wood burner while Felix told them stories about his latest business ventures. He'd tried seaweed farming in Palawan for a while, he said; and when that hadn't worked out, he'd exported clapped out Singaporean taxis to Indonesia. He'd make a fortune, somebody had told him.

He hadn't.

'You should settle down,' Mum said severely. 'Get a proper job.'

Felix roared with laughter. 'Me? Get a proper job? I'm going to retire!'

'Felix, you're far too young to retire!' Dad exclaimed. 'And anyway, you haven't got any money.'

Felix paused. A slow grin spread across his face. 'Who says I don't have any money?'

He reached into a pocket and took out a small black bag. He opened it carefully, and handed it to Dad, who peered inside.

After a moment or two, Dad looked up. He wore a strange expression. 'Where did you get this?' he asked.

'I found it.'

'What do you mean, you *found* it?'

'What is it?' Hanna, Ned, and Jik chorused, unable to contain their curiosity any longer. 'Tell us what it is!'

'Can I show them?' Dad asked.

Felix nodded.

The children crowded round and peered into the bag. Mum got up to join them. They gasped in amazement.

It was full of gold—thousands of tiny specks of it, each about the size of a grain of sand. It gleamed richly in the firelight. 'Is it real?' Ned asked in an awestruck voice.

'Completely real. I've just had it tested in London. It's one hundred per cent pure.'

'It must be worth a bomb!' Hanna said.

Felix paused. Smiled. 'It's worth . . . quite a lot of money. There's more where it came from.'

'And where's that?' Mum asked.

Felix looked serious. 'I must ask you to swear never to tell anybody what I'm going to tell you now.'

'We swear!' said Hanna, Ned, and Jik excitedly.

'How about you, Lin? Nick?'

Mum and Dad nodded.

'OK, I'll tell you. It comes from a small river, far up in the interior of the Borneo rainforest. It takes days—weeks—to reach it by boat and on foot. But when you do, the gold's just there, waiting to be collected by anybody who wants it.'

'You mean it's just lying about?' Hanna asked, disbelievingly.

'It's mixed up with the sand and mud of the river bed, but it's easy enough to extract. And there's lots of it.'

Jik gave a long, low whistle. 'Jumping jelly-beans!' he exclaimed. Jumping jellybeans was *the* very latest Jik phrase.

Everybody sat down again. Felix carefully sealed the bag and replaced it in his pocket.

'Why are you telling us this, Felix?' Mum asked. She sounded highly suspicious.

'Because I need a partner. I can't get the gold out on my own. I need somebody I can trust to help me. Strictly fifty-fifty . . . '

'NO!' Mum's reply came out as a shout. 'No, no, no, no, no! Nick's not getting involved in this! He's got a family. He's got far too much to do here!'

'You might let him answer for himself,' Felix said mildly.

'Why should I? He's stupid enough to say yes!'

There was an embarrassed silence. After a while, Dad said, 'I think you kids should go to bed.'

'But Dad,' Ned protested.

'Go to bed! Right now!'

The three children listened from upstairs as the argument raged on, long into the night. Judging by the chink of glasses there was quite a lot of whisky being drunk. When Hanna got up in the morning, a single glance at Mum's hollow eyes told her which way the decision had gone.

He'd give it three months, Dad said, and if things didn't work out, he'd come home. Charlie, his assistant, and a new boy called Darren could keep the thatching business running while he was gone. The children were to look after Mum, and do what they were told. Saying goodbye at Heathrow was like attending a funeral.

He called them from Singapore, where he changed planes, and then from Sangabera, the capital of East Borneo. After that, there was silence. The family was expecting it—there were no phone masts upriver where Dad had gone, and their radio was only for emergencies. Every night Hanna found herself praying that he was safe.

A month passed. Two. Winter gradually turned into spring. Then, one morning, a call came from the Foreign Office in London. Loggers had found a body floating in the Kerai River in Central Borneo.

Documents on the corpse had shown that it was Felix.

And Dad had been arrested and charged with his murder.

It was like the worst nightmare ever. Dad was being held in a high security jail in Sangabera. Conditions were very bad. He was being interrogated daily, though he continued to protest his innocence. The man from the Foreign Office advised Mum to fly out immediately.

She wanted to go alone, but the children insisted on coming with her. She'd need their help and support, Hanna told her—and besides, they wanted to see Dad—*needed* to see him. Reluctantly, Mum agreed.

Their flight—halfway round the world— seemed endless. They were met at Sangabera airport by a Mr Bennett from the British Embassy and by a young defence lawyer called Miss Wiyati who spoke excellent English. Miss Wiyati seemed very confident that Dad would soon be freed.

Hanna, Ned, and Jik were not allowed to visit Dad in prison, so Mum went to see him alone. She returned to their hotel room in tears. He was being held in a tiny cell with nine other men, most of whom were drug addicts, she told them. There were no beds, so he had to sleep on the bare concrete floor. The only toilet facilities were a bucket.

'What did he say about Felix?' Ned asked anxiously.

Mum dabbed at her eyes. 'He doesn't know what happened to him. They'd found quite a lot of gold, and Dad was taking it downriver to one of the Chinese dealers here in Sangabera. The boat he was travelling in broke down at a place called Long Gia, and he was stranded for over a week. He was still there when the police came and arrested him.They seemed to think that the gold he was carrying was proof that he'd murdered Felix.'

'But that's stupid!' Hanna protested.

'Of course it's stupid! Felix had stayed behind to guard the camp. News about the gold must have spread somehow. Dad said they'd seen strangers hanging around recently.'

'The police should go and look for *them*!' Ned said, furious.

'That's what Dad told them, but they wouldn't listen. They kept trying to make him confess.'

'That's because they've got no dam evidence!' Jik said.

Hanna started to remind him not to say 'dam', but stopped herself. It didn't matter. Nothing mattered except getting Dad out of that terrible prison. 'Miss Wiyati is right, is she?' she asked. 'Dad *will* get set free?'

Mum forced a smile onto her face. 'Of course he will! As Jik says, they've got no proper evidence. The trial starts on Monday. The whole thing is just a formality . . . '

3

The Cobra

The gunman grinned at them again. A gold tooth gleamed in the sunlight. The children glanced around, but escape was impossible. Even if they'd known where to run to, they didn't dare risk a bullet in their back. 'What do you want?' Ned stammered.

The man didn't answer. He passed the gun slowly from hand to hand, as if trying to guess its weight. Eventually he looked up. 'They're very stupid,' he said.

'Who are?' Hanna asked.

'My friends in uniform. They make a lot of noise, and catch nobody. Myself, I am silent—as silent and as deadly as a cobra. And when I attack . . . pow! It's all over!'

His empty hand shot out, imitating a cobra strike. The children lurched backwards in alarm. The gunman roared with laughter. He seemed to be enjoying himself hugely.

'Are you police?' Jik asked, eyeing the gun.

'I am Intel. You heard of Intel?'

'It's something inside a computer?' Hanna ventured.

Another burst of laughter. 'Not that! I am—how do you say it—secret service—FBI—detective.'

'That's three things,' Ned pointed out.

'I am everything rolled into one thing! My name is Dodi. I was in the courtroom this morning when your father was sentenced to death.'

Sentenced to death.

Hanna flinched. For the first time the full horror of those dreadful words struck home. Up till now she'd been telling herself that it was impossible for Dad to be executed for something he hadn't done. But deep inside she knew it wasn't. Even back home, even in England, things sometimes went wrong, and innocent people got put in prison for years. Many of them got pardoned eventually, and released. But you couldn't be pardoned or released if you'd been shot. There was no way of bringing a dead body back to life.

'What do you want?' she demanded, desperately trying to control her swirling thoughts.

'To help you.'

'Why?'

'Because I believe your father is not guilty of this murder, and I want to catch the people who are.'

Ned's face brightened. 'You really mean that?'

Dodi looked hurt. 'Would I say such a thing if I did not mean it?'

'We don't know,' Hanna told him coldly. 'We don't know anything about you.'

Despite his apparent friendliness there was something about this man she didn't like. Perhaps it was because of what he'd said about being a cobra. She could picture him with a scaly snake's tail and a flickering, forked tongue.

Ned and Jik had no such inhibitions. 'Do you *really* think you can find out what happened?' Ned asked.

Dodi nodded. 'Of course.'

'How?'

'By using this!' he said. 'And this!' He tapped his nose and then his forehead. 'I use my nostrils to sniff out clues, and my brain to solve them. I use— how do you say it in English—*loggik*?'

'Logic,' Hanna said coldly.

'Exactly! My brain is like a supercomputer.'

'Jumping jellybeans!' Jik said, impressed.

A puzzled look came onto Dodi's face. 'What are these jellybeans you are telling me about?'

'Just an expression,' Ned replied hastily. 'Where did you get your gun?'

'It is Intel detective gun. With improvements.'

'What improvements?'

21

'I make it longer so it can shoot more straight. I am a brilliant marksman.'

'You seem to be a brilliant everything,' Hanna said.

Dodi didn't respond to the sarcasm in her voice. He was peering down the alley. 'We must go,' he said. 'Soon many people will come here to eat food. They will ask questions if they see me with white kids. Questions I do not want to answer. Come!' He got to his feet and set off swiftly towards the main road.

The boys made to follow him, but Hanna grabbed their arms and held them back. 'How do we know we can trust you?' she called out.

Dodi stopped, turned. 'Only I can find out the truth. Only I can get your father set free. If you want that, you must trust me. If not, I say bye-bye right now!'

Hanna sucked in a deep breath. If they stayed where they were they'd be picked up by the police, sooner or later. They had no choice *but* to trust him.

'OK,' she said, reluctantly. 'We trust you.'

'Good!' The detective set off again at high speed.

'Where are we going?' Ned asked, as they struggled to keep up.

'To my house. You will be safe there. Then I make arrangements.'

'What arrangements?'

'You ask too many questions. Just follow!'

It was mid-day. After the storm, the heat had returned, and the sun blazed down from a cloudless sky. Soon they were drenched in sweat. Dodi led them through a maze of tiny streets, each one seemingly more smelly and garbage-strewn than the last. Eventually he stopped at a small wooden shack, with a huge rusting TV satellite dish bolted to its roof. 'This is my house,' he announced. 'Please, to enter.'

He pushed at the door.

It opened into a small, dark room, with no furniture except a large television set. A single window let in a glimmer of light. There was a strong smell of human excrement. He stuck his head through a rear door. *'Nenek!'*

There was a muttered reply. Moments later an ancient woman shuffled into the room. She was wearing a faded sarong, and was bent almost double. She looked like a witch from one of Hanna's old storybooks. 'This is my *nenek*—my grandmother,' Dodi announced. 'Please sit. She will get you water to drink. I must go to make arrangements.'

He said something to her in Indonesian and followed her out. The door swung shut behind them.

Apprehensive, the children squatted in the

23

middle of the floor and waited. After a while they heard the sound of Dodi's voice from the next room. He was talking to somebody on the telephone. 'What's he saying?' Hanna whispered to Jik.

The Sea Gypsy boy crept close to the door and listened intently. 'He telephone to somebody called *Tuan Besar*. That mean Big Boss,' he whispered. 'More than that I cannot tell. He speak too dam quiet.'

He scurried back to Hanna and Ned as the door creaked open again. It was the old woman. She was carrying a tray containing three plastic cups, a jug of water and a small plate of dry crackers.

She put the tray down on the floor. '*Makan*,' she said, pointing at the plate. 'Eat.' She went out again.

They sipped at the water, which they hoped was boiled, but left the crackers untouched. All three of them had lost their appetites. There were shouts from the street outside, the ringing of a hand-bell. Somebody was selling noodles. The vendor didn't stop at their door.

Dodi was on the phone for a long time. Eventually he came back into the room. He wore a satisfied expression. 'I fix everything,' he said. 'Tomorrow we go.'

'Go where?' Hanna asked.

'Upriver. To find out who kill your father's friend.'

'But what about Mum and Dad?' Ned asked anxiously. 'They'll be worried about us.'

'I tell you, I fix everything. Your mother is in the women's jail. They keep her there for one month. I get word to her that you are OK and she is not to worry. I get word to your father also. I have many connections. Everywhere there are people who want to help me.'

He picked up the plate of crackers, offered them round. 'You not like?'

'We're not hungry,' Hanna told him.

Dodi grinned. 'I like!' He stuffed several into his mouth, crunched them up. 'You are very lucky kids,' he announced, spraying crumbs. 'Very lucky—to have Dodi as your good friend!'

4

Mr Mouth

It was a terrible night. Confined to the cramped, stuffy front room of Dodi's house, except for visits to what had to be the smelliest, most disgusting toilet in the entire world, the children might have been able to snatch a little sleep on the mats they were given, if it hadn't been for the TV. Dodi switched it on as dusk fell, and it stayed on until the early hours of the morning with its volume turned up to maximum.

It began with Indonesian soap operas, most of them featuring overweight actors in posh houses, and ended with a football match—Manchester United against a team from Germany. Dodi seemed to know everything about the players— how many goals they'd scored, what their trans- fer fees had been—constantly firing questions at poor Ned, who'd made the big mistake of admit- ting that he supported Liverpool. When United scored, Dodi leapt to his feet, shouting 'Goooooal!', and capered about like a three year old. He'd learned to speak English by watching

TV, he told the children at half time, and now he could speak it better than anybody who'd been born in London. Even Jik, who'd been casting admiring glances at him from the back of the room, found that hard to believe.

When the set had finally been switched off, and the three children were alone together at last, sleep still failed to come to Hanna. Every time she closed her eyes, she was back in the crowded courtroom listening to the judge give his terrible verdict: *'Nicholas James Bailey, you will be executed by firing squad four weeks from this date . . .'*

Four weeks.

She did some quick maths in her head. That was twenty-eight days from now. Even if Dodi was everything he boasted he was—even if he *was* the greatest detective in the world—how could they possibly hope to find out the truth in such a short time, in one of the most remote and dangerous places on earth?

She glanced at Ned. He too was awake, his eyes shining in the reflected light from the street outside. She stretched out a hand, placed it gently on his. He looked across at her and gave a small, sad smile. 'We'll get Dad free,' she told him determinedly. 'I don't know how we'll do it, but we will!'

They lay in silence for a while, lost in their own

27

thoughts. Hanna was missing Dad more than she could have ever believed possible. It was like an acute pain that wouldn't go away.

It was Ned who eventually spoke. 'What did he say to you?' he whispered.

'Who?'

'Dad. I saw him saying something to you before the police took him away. While all that fighting was going on.'

Hanna thought back. He'd said just two words—that much she remembered. And he'd said them over and over again. But what on earth were they? She racked her brains.

She was about to tell Ned that there'd been too much noise, too much confusion, when suddenly, unexpectedly, her mind cleared. She was back in the pandemonium of the courtroom once more, fighting to get to Dad. He was turning towards her, as if in slow motion. She could see his lips move. She could read what they were saying . . .

Some beer . . .

He was asking for *some beer . . .*

'*Beer?*' Ned sounded incredulous when she told him.

'That's what I think he said.'

'But Dad doesn't drink beer—at least not Borneo beer! He says it fills him up with gas!'

'Maybe he's changed his mind.'

Ned snorted. 'I doubt it. You know what Dad's like!'

Hanna tried to conjure up her father's face again, but the vision had gone. Ned was right. Dad *hated* local beer. And even if he loved it, why would he mention it in the courtroom when there was so little time and so many more important things to say—like the fact that he was innocent; and how much he loved them all?

She'd got it wrong, she reluctantly decided. Her brain was playing tricks on her. She tried to explain this to Ned, but he ignored her and turned to face the wall.

She must have slept eventually, because she was woken by the wail of a muezzin from a nearby mosque, calling the faithful to morning prayer. A cockerel crowed in somebody's back yard. As if on cue, Dodi came bustling in with glasses of hot sweet tea, urging the children to get up and get going. They must hurry, he told them.

It was still quite dark when they left the house, threading their way silently between locked and shuttered warehouses, down towards the river. They could smell the Kerai long before they reached it. It had a sour, vinegary tang which for some reason reminded Hanna of pickled onions.

This far downstream, the great river, which formed one of the main highways into the heart of Borneo, was a poisonous cocktail of untreated sewage and pollution from the coal mines and sawmills that lined its banks.

There was a boat waiting at the end of a wooden jetty. It was long and narrow, with four large outboard engines mounted on its stern. It had a name painted on its side: *Maidah*. It was being swiftly loaded with sacks of cement, bundles of plastic drainage pipes, and drums of diesel fuel by four muscular youths.

Supervising the operation, issuing a constant stream of sharp orders, was a small, plump man, with tiny, glittering eyes and a straggly moustache. He looked like an irritable seal. He acknowledged Dodi with a nod, scanned the children up and down as if they were awkward items of cargo to be loaded, then turned his attention back to the boat.

'This man is Pak Mulut,' Dodi told the children as they waited to board. 'He is the godfather of the whole Kerai River. His name means Mr Mouth. If you do things he doesn't like, or say things he doesn't like, he'll eat you up.'

'He's a cannibal?' Jik asked in a quavering voice.

Dodi let out a snort of laughter. 'Oh no. He's much more dangerous than that!'

The last of the cargo was finally carried on board and secured, and a tattered tarpaulin spread over it. Pak Mulut lifted up a corner, beckoned to the children. 'Come!' he said, in heavily accented English, pointing at the space beneath.

Dodi pushed them into it.

It was dark under the tarpaulin, and the fumes from the fuel drums made Hanna's eyes water. She tried to settle herself, but only succeeded in squashing Jik's legs painfully against the sharp ends of the drainage pipes. Ned, too, seemed seriously uncomfortable. How many hours would this cramped, smelly journey take?

How many *days*?

She leaned forward to ask Dodi, whose back was just visible through a split in the tarpaulin, but if he made a reply she didn't hear it. At a sharp command from Pak Mulut, the youths, who had finished loading, started the engines and the boat swung swiftly away from the jetty.

They seemed to be travelling at high speed, but when Ned eased back the cover to check, Hanna saw that they were actually moving quite slowly, battling against a violent current. Heading upstream, they zigzagged between lines of moored barges, each loaded with a small mountain of dusty coal.

They passed under a bridge.

There were several bridges across the river in Sangabera, Hanna remembered. She was trying to work out which one this was when the tarpaulin was jerked painfully down over her head. 'Stay hiding!' Dodi hissed. 'Everywhere police are looking. If they see your white faces, they will send a boat to stop us!'

After a while it began to rain. Not a violent tropical downpour like the day before, but a grey, soaking drizzle that reminded Hanna of home. As the rainwater dribbled through the rips and cuts in the tarpaulin, her hopes began to give way to despair. They'd had adventures in the past— dangerous adventures—but somehow she'd never felt as helpless as she did now.

They were at the mercy of an armed man they'd met just hours earlier, and knew nothing about. Why was he so interested in finding out about Dad? What was in it for him? And who exactly was this 'Big Boss' Jik had heard him talking to?

She tried to come up with answers, but failed. She felt as helpless as Dad in his prison cell. She couldn't stop her tears adding to the trickle of rainwater on her cheeks.

About an hour into the journey, the tarpaulin was suddenly jerked back. 'It is safe. Now you come out,' Dodi told them.

Rubbing their aching limbs, the children stood

up and stared around. Even this far from Sangabera, the river was still wide. Millions of gallons of chocolate-brown, silt-laden water were swirling past them on their way to the sea.

The rain had stopped, and a pale sun had come out, lighting up a devastated landscape. Once, Hanna knew, huge forest trees had grown down to the water's edge on each side of the river. But now there was just tangled scrub, interspersed with patches of bare red earth, and straggly, unsanitary-looking villages. Drifting downstream past them, heading for the sawmills and waiting freighters, were hundreds of newly-felled tree trunks, lashed together to form vast floating rafts. On them were crude huts with tarpaulin roofs where people were living. The smoke from their cooking fires spiralled up into the midday sky.

Hanna caught Ned's eye. They'd learned about the rainforest at school, how it was being destroyed by illegal logging. But it was quite different seeing the results with your own eyes. She remembered Dad saying that within a few years there wouldn't be any forest left in Borneo.

When she mentioned this to Dodi, he shrugged. 'People need work. Logging gives them work.'

She couldn't think of an answer to that.

All day long the *Maidah* fought its way

upstream. They passed several small riverside villages, but stopped at none of them. Pak Mulut spent the entire journey hunched morosely in the bows, talking to nobody. When the rain stopped and the sun came out, he put on a wide, conical hat, decorated with intricate embroidery and strips of brightly-coloured cloth. 'He looks like a posh lady at a wedding,' Ned whispered to Hanna and Jik.

The three children smiled at that, but none of them dared laugh out loud.

There was a piece of string lying in the bottom of the boat. It must have fallen off one of the sacks. Trying to banish her gloomy thoughts, Hanna picked it up and twisted it round her fingers, as if she was playing cat's-cradle. As she did so she suddenly realized that it was the answer to a problem that had been bothering her all morning. There were twenty-eight—no, *twenty-seven*—days left before the date of Dad's execution: twenty-seven days to come up with the evidence that would set him free. It would be unforgivable to become confused and lose track of time.

She slipped the string from her fingers, and carefully tied twenty-seven knots in it, spacing them evenly along its length. Every morning, as soon as she woke up, she would untie one, and then count how many days remained. It was the perfect solution! She pushed the string into her pocket, and leaned back against the side of the boat.

It made her feel just a little less helpless.

5

Voices in the Night

It was late afternoon when they finally stopped. They'd reached Long Gia, the last big settlement on the Kerai before the rapids began. Pak Mulut had a house in the village. They would spend the night there.

While they were climbing up the steep steps from the floating jetty where the *Maidah* had been moored, Hanna suddenly remembered that Long Gia was the place where Dad had been arrested while he was travelling back to Sangabera with his gold. It was here, too, that Felix's body had been brought to be indentified, and where he was buried. She mentioned it to Ned. This was an excellent place to start looking for clues! They must keep their eyes and ears open at all times.

Long Gia consisted of a single, dusty street, lined with scruffy wooden houses and small open-fronted shops. It was crowded with villagers, young and old, sitting on verandas and front steps, chatting and relaxing. Mats were laid out everywhere, spread with newly-harvested hill rice drying in the evening sunshine.

Hanna was prepared for people's curiosity— but not their fear. When they spotted the three of them with Dodi and Pak Mulut, there were audible gasps of shock. Conversations were quickly abandoned, and children sharply called in from play, as people scurried inside their houses. Soon only a few stray dogs and chickens were left in the street.

'What's going on?' Ned asked, as unnerved as Hanna was by what was happening. 'Why are these people so scared of us?'

Pak Mulut turned towards the children. 'Take no notice,' he said, in surprisingly good English. 'The people here are from the jungle. They're very stupid. They believe many stupid things!'

The boatman's house was on a ridge overlooking the river. It was a large, low, wooden building surrounded by mango and rambutan trees. There was a wide veranda at the front, and several thatched outbuildings to the rear. He pointed to a bench on the veranda and the children sat down. Then he and Dodi disappeared inside.

They were left alone for a long time. After a while, the smell of cooking wafted towards them on the evening air. It reminded the children of how hungry they were. Apart from a few tiny stale cakes handed out by Dodi at lunchtime, they'd had nothing all day.

Ned was just remarking how he could eat a horse, when Jik suddenly stiffened. 'Look,' he exclaimed.

He was pointing at a gap in the straggly hibiscus hedge that surrounded the house. Peering through it at them were two small brown faces. Hanna recognized them as village boys they'd seen earlier.

Jik glanced round quickly, then called out softly: '*Mari sini!*'

The boys shrank back into the shadows.

'What did you say to them?' Hanna asked.

'I ask them to come here. I want to find out why everybody is so dam frighten of us.'

'Tell them we won't hurt them—' Ned began.

He didn't finish. Barking furiously, four large hunting dogs bounded out of the house and raced towards the intruders.

The boys tried to get away, but they were too slow. The dogs were onto them in seconds, knocking them to the ground. They'd have been seriously injured if Pak Mulut hadn't come onto the veranda and called the animals off. He strode across to the sobbing pair, hauled them to their feet, cuffed them around the ears, and sent them scurrying back towards the village. One of them had blood trickling down his leg from a bite wound.

'You talk to nobody while you're here!' he told Hanna, Ned, and Jik angrily. '*Nobody!* You understand?'

They nodded numbly and he went back inside.

Night fell. A generator started up somewhere behind the house. Dim lights flickered on. Still sitting on their bench, not daring to move, the children slapped at mosquitoes and stared out into the darkness. They felt a very long way from home.

Eventually, Dodi came to the door and beckoned them inside. He handed them over to a frightened-looking servant woman who led them to a ground-floor bedroom at the back of the house. There were three grubby mattresses heaped one on top of the other, and no pillows. The children were given a sarong each, and shown where the bathroom was. It contained a large concrete tank filled with river water. There was a plastic scoop for ladling it over themselves.

Hanna bathed first, then the boys. They rinsed out their grubby clothes and hung them up to dry. Afterwards, wearing their sarongs, they were escorted to the main room of the house.

Their jaws dropped in amazement as they entered. It looked more like a museum than a living room. Lining its walls were dozens of intricately carved and decorated spears and shields. Exquisite feathered headdresses hung from hooks.

Pak Mulut was sitting at a low table with Dodi. For the first time since they'd met him that morning, his face creased into a smile. He spread his hands proudly. 'You like my collection? These things are made by the Kenyah people. They are the fiercest and bravest of all Borneo warriors.' He puffed out his chest. 'I am Kenyah!'

The children didn't know how to respond.

He stood up, went over to a glass-topped cabinet. He unlocked it, and took something out. He brought it across. '*This* is what makes us brave! It is called a *mandau.*'

He was holding a sword. It had an intricately-carved deer horn handle, and was tassled with what looked like human hair. Its short, notched blade gleamed in the electric light. He swished it through the air like a Chinese swordfighter. 'One strike from this and your head will tumble from your body!'

He offered it to Ned. 'You want to try?'

Ned shook his head violently.

Pak Mulut chuckled. 'You are like my good friend Dodi here! He also is Kenyah, but he does not like swords. He is modern man. He prefers a gun!'

He carefully returned the sword to its case, then

turned and clapped his hands loudly. 'Now we eat!' he exclaimed. 'Come, sit with us!'

Shortly afterwards the servant woman came into the room with a pot of boiled rice. She was followed by a young girl carrying a bowl of stewed fish. 'This is *ikan patin*,' Pak Mulut said, while the women served them. 'Kerai River catfish. Very tasty. Please, eat!'

The children were given water to drink, but Pak Mulut waved the jug away when it was offered to him. Instead, he poured himself and Dodi generous helpings of what looked like lemonade from a plastic bottle. Jik knew what it was. 'They drink *arak*,' he whispered to Hanna. 'Like vodka, only even more strong. Make you goddam drunk!'

So that must be what had caused Pak Mulut's change of mood! Somehow it made him seem even more scary.

The food was delicious, and despite their nervousness, all three children had second helpings. Dodi and Pak Mulut chatted to each other in a language Jik didn't understand—presumably Kenyah—and drank steadily. Even though they laughed a lot, Hanna had a strong feeling that the two men didn't like each other.

She was puzzled by Dodi. He was supposed to be a detective, but so far he'd made no attempt to look for clues.

She plucked up the courage to ask him why not.

He snorted derisively. 'The people here are very stupid—Pak Mulut has already told you that. We waste our time to talk to them. Later, we will find good clues.'

'Where?'

'Upriver, past the rapids, at the place where your father found his gold.'

'How can you be so certain?' Ned asked.

'Because I will sniff them out like one of Pak's hunting dogs!' He made a howling noise, stuck out his tongue and panted.

Pak Mulut roared with laughter, slapping at his knee, as if it was the funniest thing he'd ever heard. 'He is a great big clown, this Dodi, no?'

The children nodded cautiously.

'So why do you not laugh?'

'We're tired,' Hanna said quickly. 'It's been a long day.'

'Then go sleep. But remember what I said. Talk to nobody!' His eyes glittered.

At the door, Ned paused, turned to Dodi. 'How did Felix die?' he asked. 'How was he killed? Nobody has ever told us.'

The detective's eyes narrowed. 'Why do you want to know?'

'Because it might be an important clue.'

'I am sorry. I cannot tell you.'

'Why not?'

'It is not right for me to do so. You are children. You are too young.'

'We're not infants!' Hanna snapped.

Dodi banged his glass down onto the table. His jovial mood had vanished. 'Out!' he snapped, pointing at the door. 'Get out now! I do not answer any more questions!'

Back in their room, the children spread out their mattresses and thumped down unhappily onto them. 'Dodi's hiding something,' Hanna said. 'I'm convinced of it! Otherwise, why would he get so angry when we asked him about Felix?'

'And why won't Pak Mulut let us talk to anybody?' Ned added. 'The people in this place *must* know something. They might be frightened, but they're *not* stupid!'

'Let's go and find out for ourselves,' Jik proposed. 'We'll wait until everybody is dam asleep . . . '

Ned shook his head violently. 'No! The dogs are on the loose. I saw them in the yard. If we try to leave the house, they'll attack us for sure.'

'So we just stay here and do nothing?'

Hanna shrugged. 'What *can* we do? We're leaving early in the morning. Dodi's right. There are bound to be clues where we're going—really good clues. Let's wait and concentrate on those.'

She yawned. What she'd said back in the living room was true. She was dead tired. And so, judging by their faces, were the boys. It was time to sleep. Tomorrow promised to be another long, difficult day.

Hanna's eyes flicked open. The singing that had woken her was coming from somewhere nearby. At first she thought it must be Pak Mulut or Dodi. They'd kept the children awake for hours, drinking *arak* and bellowing out Indonesian pop songs in loud, tuneless voices.

But this was no pop song.

This was a sad, lilting lament in a language she didn't understand.

And it was being sung by a woman.

Her gaze switched to the only patch of light in the darkness of the bedroom—a small, square window that looked out onto a moonlit courtyard at the rear of the house. There was no glass in its frame, just fine-meshed netting to keep out the mosquitoes. As she watched, she saw the clear silhouette of a woman's head pass by; then return again a short while later.

Trying not to disturb the boys, she crept to the window, and peered through it.

The courtyard backed onto the kitchen. It was

littered with garbage—broken plastic boxes, rusting tin cans, and empty rice-sacks. In its centre was a scrawny papaya tree.

The woman was doing a slow circuit of the tree, singing the same sad, gentle song over and over again. She had greying hair gathered into little-girl bunches at the sides of her head, and was wearing a stained, floral-patterned dress. She was holding a pink plastic hand-mirror, and was staring into it intently as she walked. Pak Mulut's four fierce dogs were crouched on the far side of the yard, their eyes following her protectively.

It was only when she finally turned towards the window that Hanna was able to see her face clearly.

She recoiled in shock. The woman's cheeks were coated with thick white make-up, which shone in the moonlight. Her eyes were crudely outlined in black. Her lips were smeared with bright red lipstick, drawn into a grotesque upward curve. She looked like a clown.

She lived here—the behaviour of the dogs confirmed that. Perhaps she knew something about Dad, Hanna found herself thinking—something important. This could be their only chance to find out.

But dare she risk calling her over?

Pak Mulut's warning about not talking to anybody was still vivid in her mind. But he was asleep now—dead drunk. So was Dodi. Their snores were echoing through the house . . .

She took a deep breath and pushed open the window.

A hinge creaked.

The dogs heard it and growled. The woman broke off from her singing, saw what was happening, and made a sharp clicking noise with her tongue. The dogs fell silent. She came up to the window and peered in. She smelt strongly of cheap perfume.

'Do you speak English?' Hanna asked her hesitantly.

The look of sadness on the woman's face was instantly replaced by one of intense joy. She reached out and stroked Hanna's hand. '*Cantek!*' she whispered. '*Cantek!*'

Hanna knew enough Indonesian to recognize the word. 'Beautiful,' she was saying. 'You are beautiful!'

Then, without warning, her expression switched again. Fear replaced the joy. '*Anak putih,*' she hissed, backing away as if she'd just seen a ghost.

The noise woke Ned and Jik. They scrambled to join Hanna at the window. The woman's terror increased when she saw them. She glanced round as if fearing attack, then opened her mouth and began to scream: *'Bahaya! Anak putih! Bahaya! Bali saleng!'*

Her voice soared into the night air.

'What's she saying?' Hanna asked Jik, terrified that she would wake Pak Mulut or Dodi.

The Sea Gypsy boy looked worried. 'She say there is big danger from something called *bali saleng*, but I don't know what this dam thing is. It's got something to do with you two being white kids.'

The woman was hysterical now, screeching the words at the top of her voice: *'Bahaya! Bali saleng! Bahaya!'*

There was a sudden commotion from the house. The young girl who'd served them with the stewed fish earlier hurried into the courtyard, fastening a sarong around herself as she did so. She shot the children an apprehensive glance, then grabbed hold of the woman. *'Nakal!'* she scolded. 'Naughty!' She dragged her quickly back inside.

The door banged shut behind them.

6

White Water

They left the house at first light, stumbling behind Dodi as he strode swiftly down the deserted main street to the river, where the *Maidah* was being loaded with more cargo—sacks of rice, this time—by Pak Mulut's men.

The boatman was back to his usual morose self, pointing at where the children were to sit as they came on board, but otherwise not acknowledging their presence. Dodi was also silent, no doubt nursing a large hangover.

The rice sacks were covered with a tarpaulin, and the children slumped down against them. At least today they wouldn't need to be covered up too.

They were exhausted. Sleep had been impossible after what had happened in the night, and they were still discussing it when Dodi had hammered on their door, ordering them to get up.

The woman in the courtyard was seriously disturbed—that much was obvious. But it didn't explain her reaction when she'd spotted them.

Why should Hanna and Ned having white skins make her so terrified? Surely she'd seen Europeans before?

And what was this mysterious *bali saleng* she'd been screaming about? Was it just the raving of a mad woman, or was there something more sinister behind it—something that might give a clue to what had really happened to Felix? There were so many questions—and no answers at all.

They'd considered asking Dodi, but decided against it. They trusted him less and less as time went on. It was better to keep quiet about it, they'd decided. With luck, the truth would eventually reveal itself.

When the cargo was finally secured, the four huge engines roared into life, and the heavily-laden boat accelerated out into the swirling river.

Dodi handed the children breakfast—portions of rice and fish from the night before, wrapped in neat banana leaf packets—and as they ate it, they watched the landscape flow by.

They passed several small Kenyah villages— each with a colourful wooden welcome arch straddling the steps leading up from the river. The carved and painted faces on them reminded Hanna of Native American totem poles. Between the villages were rice fields, hacked out of the forest. In some of them, farmers were already at work, harvesting the ripe grain, chopping the ears from their stalks with small t-shaped knives, before throwing them into baskets hung on their backs. Other farmers were waiting on landing stages to be picked up and taken to their fields by the numerous motorized canoes that were buzzing backwards and forwards across the river. When they spotted the children, their faces registered the same mixture of surprise and fear as the people of Long Gia.

Beyond the villages, the rice fields stopped, and the forest began—scruffy secondary jungle, with a few tall trees still standing. Apart from the occasional longboat like theirs—all of which were heading downstream—they were now alone on the river. There were numerous logging camps; muddy clearings scattered with barrack-like huts. Massive yellow grab-tractors twisted and roared as they hoisted and stacked huge tree trunks that were waiting to be rafted downstream.

Hour succeeded hour. Lulled by the motion, and the cooling breeze, the children felt increasingly sleepy.

Their eyes closed.

Moments later, they were wide open again.

The *Maidah* had rounded a sharp bend and was accelerating straight and hard into the first of the great Kerai rapids. The river, smooth and wide up to now, was blasting between two vertical walls of rock with the power and venom of a giant water cannon.

Their engines screaming, the four drivers pointed the boat at the centre of the torrent. Pak Mulut, crouched in the bow, his head bent against the lashing spray, gave a series of rapid arm-signals, not taking his eyes off the river for one second. The drivers responded instantly to his instructions, aiming the craft unerringly between vicious-looking spurs of rock that threatened to rip the bottom out of it at any moment.

The rapid was just the first of a whole series, stacked one above the other like a vast watery staircase, each one wilder than the last. His arms revolving like windmills, Pak Mulut directed the boat through them, screaming insults at his drivers if they so much as touched a submerged rock.

'How does he know which way to steer?' Ned asked Dodi in awe, when they eventually emerged unscathed into a quiet section of stream.

The detective shrugged. 'I told you. Pak Mulut is the godfather of the Kerai. He knows this river like his own child.'

More sets of rapids followed, each one heralded by a rainbow arc of spray. Some were wide and shallow, others narrow and steep. They all had names. One was called 'The Tortoise'—the most dangerous of all. Another, *'Take Your Time'*. A third, *'Goodbye, come back soon.'* Unerringly, Pak Mulut piloted the huge boat up through the lot of them.

The logging camps were gone now—the rapids were far too wild and narrow to float big tree trunks downstream through them—and the forest was completely untouched. Trees, hung with cable-like creepers, and decorated here and there with vivid orange and yellow flowers, soared sixty or seventy metres into the pale tropical sky; with the occasional giant stretching above even those. Troops of monkeys, drinking at the water's edge, scurried for safety as the boat powered past. Huge white butterflies fluttered and flapped above the forest canopy like wind-blown handkerchiefs. The children stared in awe as they penetrated further and further into the untouched wilderness.

The journey seemed never-ending. That night, and for two nights afterwards, they slept in primitive wooden shacks clinging to the steep valley sides. The diet was monotonous in the extreme: boiled rice or instant noodles, only occasionally cheered up by a few cooked fern leaves, or a piece of dried fish. As Ned pointed out forcefully after his sixth identical meal, it was even worse than school food.

They got to know the four drivers. Their names were Kiki, Lucas, Karmin, and Bili. They turned out to be Pak Mulut's sons. The children particularly liked Bili, who had a cheeky grin, and was always ready with a funny gesture or a joke.

Towards the middle of the third day they left the Kerai, and steered into a large tributary called the Barang. They could go no further up the main river, Dodi told the children. There were huge rapids and waterfalls that would defeat even Pak Mulut. The new river was almost as big, but less dangerous. There were settlements upstream, with people who might have important information about Dad.

Later that afternoon they saw the wild pigs.

There was a whole family of them—including several tiny striped piglets—swimming across the river, battling against the current as they went.

Pak Mulut spotted them first from his perch in the bow, and pointed them out.

His sons let out a whoop of glee, and swung the boat towards the animals. They began to panic, squealing with terror, desperate to get away, but unable to swim fast enough. 'Leave them alone or they'll drown!' Hanna yelled, horrified, as the babies were swamped by the wash from the engines.

Nobody listened to her.

As they closed in on the largest of the pigs, Dodi

reached for his shoulder bag, took out his gun, and aimed.

A shot cracked out.

There was a shriek of agony as the bullet slammed into the animal's neck. It began to sink. Not bothering to check whether it was alive or dead, Bili grabbed a boat-hook and dragged it to the side. Lucas took a sharp knife from his belt, gripped it by its ears, raised its head and slit its throat.

Instantly, the river ran red with blood. The tiny piglets were caught in it, coughing, squealing, as they struggled frantically towards the far shore.

Dodi took aim again.

'No!'

It was Jik. He was furious. 'Kill what you need, but don't kill any more! Otherwise the ghosts of this dam place will kill us too!'

He tried to grab the gun from the detective's hands, but Ned held him back.

Hanna glanced up at Dodi's face. It was as if a mask had slipped momentarily. His eyes had narrowed to tiny slits.

They were the eyes of a snake, venomous and lethal.

The look was gone as quickly as it had come. The detective laughed, slapped Jik on the back. 'You're right!' he said, over-loudly. 'We've got plenty of meat for now—and there's more where that came from!'

As the last of the terrified animals struggled ashore and disappeared into the undergrowth, he reloaded his gun and slipped it back into his bag.

7

The Blood Collector

That night there was no hut. Instead, they camped on a rocky spur of land stretching out into the river. Kiki, Lucas, Karmin, and Bili draped tarpaulins over poles to make tents and secured them with heavy rocks. A fire of driftwood was built and lit, and large chunks of pork were roasted on bamboo spits.

Despite the horrible way it had been killed, Hanna found the meat delicious; and after everybody had eaten, the remaining pork was cut into strips and put onto wooden racks to smoke slowly over the embers of the fire until morning.

It was too early to go to sleep, so the men sat around, smoking clove-scented cigarettes and drinking *arak*.

Pak Mulut became increasingly unhappy as the alcohol took effect. Something was obviously troubling him deeply. On one occasion he spoke vehemently to Dodi in the Kenyah language, pointing downriver, but was sharply rebuffed. Despite all the talk about him being the godfather, there was little doubt about who was really in charge of the expedition.

Unable to follow the conversation, Hanna, Ned, and Jik sat apart from the others on a broad, flat rock that was still warm from the day's sunshine. They talked about Mum and Dad mostly, worrying about how they were surviving in prison. They hoped desperately that Dodi had really managed to get a message through to them as he'd promised. Fireflies danced at the side of the stream— tiny green specks of ghostly light; and every so often a huge jungle moth would spiral down, attracted by the light of the fire. If somebody had told them they'd reached the end of the world and were about to fall off the edge, they would have had no trouble in believing it.

Unable to keep their eyes open, the children slumped tiredly against each other. Surely the men would stop drinking soon and they could all get some rest?

They were on the verge of sleep when the scream came. It ripped through the night like a chain-saw; high-pitched, sharp-edged, filling the valley with its echo.

It came again.

And a third time.

It sounded like death itself.

They scrambled across to where the men were

sitting. 'What make that dam noise?' Jik demanded, badly spooked.

Pak Mulut exchanged glances with his sons, but said nothing.

It was Dodi who eventually spoke. 'Maybe it is a *bali saleng*,' he said quietly.

The *bali saleng* again! Perhaps they could now find out what it was. Hanna plucked up the courage to ask.

'It is a very dangerous thing,' Dodi told her. 'Some people say it is human. Others say it is a demon.'

'We don't believe in demons,' Ned said quickly. 'So it must be human!'

Dodi ignored him. He beckoned the children across to where he was sitting. He raised his chin and pointed at his throat. Just visible in the flickering firelight was a jagged scar. 'A *bali saleng* did this,' he said quietly. 'I was a small boy in my village when one of them came to take my blood. If my father had not heard my cries and chased it away, I would have been dead.'

Jik's eyes widened. 'Do they drink blood? Like vampires?'

Dodi shook his head. 'They don't *drink* it, they *steal* it. They are blood collectors. They collect the blood to sell it. Big companies—oil companies, timber companies—pay much money for it.

58

Thousands of dollars. Especially for the blood of young children.'

Hanna was aghast. 'But why?'

'To bring them good fortune and prosperity. When they dig the foundations of a new factory or office block, the owners always make an offering to *Bali Tanah,* the earth demon. Of course they say it is buffalo blood they use, or sheep's blood, but that is not the truth.'

There was a stunned silence, broken only by the rasp of cicadas and the chirping of tree frogs. The three children glanced around fearfully. 'What do these *bali saleng* look like?' Hanna just managed to ask.

'They take many forms. Their favourite form is a Kenyah warrior. But sometimes they take the form of a leopard, or even a white man.'

'Do they ever take the form of a white *child*?'

This time it was Pak Mulut who answered. 'Why do you say that?'

Hanna hesitated. Dare she tell him what the mad woman had said to them back in Long Gia?

She had nothing to lose, she decided.

Instead of the anger she'd anticipated, the boatman reacted with sadness to her story. 'This woman is my wife,' he said. 'Her name is Maidah. My boat is named after her. She is . . . much troubled. There is talk in the village that the *bali saleng*

59

now takes the shape of white children. Maidah has obviously heard this talk.'

'Was that why everybody was so frightened of us when we arrived?' Ned asked.

Pak Mulut nodded. 'It is why I say to you to talk to nobody, and why I let loose my dogs. Some people may want to do you harm. Even try to kill you. You are my guest. I cannot permit that . . .'

Another scream.

Heads jerked in the direction of the sound.

Dodi turned to the children. His face was eerily lit by the flickering firelight. 'You asked me how Felix died. Now I will tell you despite your young age. I think it was a *bali saleng* who killed him. He was a big man. He had much blood. It was worth many dollars. He was in the forest alone. It would have been easy for a *bali saleng* to catch him and cut his throat.'

'So why didn't you tell us this before?' Ned demanded.

'I have already explained: it was because I did not wish to frighten you. Many people—many children—are very afraid of *bali saleng*. They have bad nightmares.'

'Is there any way we can prove it was one of these blood collectors?' Hanna asked, her hopes rising.

Dodi shook his head. 'The body was in the river

for several days before it was found. Parts of it were . . . missing.'

'*Missing*?'

'There are rapids, waterfalls, sharp rocks. It was smashed to a pulp. And there are crocodiles.'

'Crocodiles! But we haven't seen any crocodiles!' Ned exclaimed.

'They are very skilled at hiding themselves, but believe me, they're here.'

'But there must be tests,' Hanna said frantically. 'Scientific tests. DNA. Even if they can't prove who did it, surely they can prove that Dad *didn't*! We must dig up the body. Get it . . . *exhumed*.'

Dodi shook his head. 'This is the tropics. By now it will have rotted. There will be no flesh left.'

'But Dad's life depends on it! He's innocent!'

The detective paused. 'Even if we could do tests—even if we could *prove* that Felix's blood had been stolen—the judge would not accept it as evidence.'

'Why not?'

'Because if he announced to the world that your father's friend had been killed by a blood-collecting demon, our nation would become a laughing stock.'

Hanna was aghast. 'Is that more important than saving an innocent man's life?'

'To our leaders, much more important. We are

61

a modern country. Modern people do not believe in demons.'

Hanna twisted towards Pak Mulut. 'What do you think?' she demanded.

'He agrees with me,' Dodi said forcefully. 'And so do his sons.'

Pak Mulut met Hanna's enquiring gaze and shrugged. His expression was blank.

'If you know all these things already, why do you bring us all the way up this goddam river?' Jik demanded.

Dodi spread his hands. 'Because I think maybe we can find other evidence. Something that the judge will accept.'

'Like what?'

'How can I know until we've found it.'

The detective stood up. Stared out into the night. For somebody confronting demons he seemed strangely relaxed. 'I think there are no more *bali saleng*,' he announced after a moment or two. 'They are gone. Now it is safe to sleep. I hope what I have just told you will not disturb you kids too much.'

Hanna *was* disturbed—but not just by Dodi's words. She was staring at his left hand, which was lit by the firelight.

The nail on his little finger was longer than the rest, and was curved into the shape of a sharp-pointed claw.

8

Stuck

The rising sun was splashing the tops of the tallest forest trees with gold as the *Maidah* set off upriver again. High above, a pair of white-headed eagles circled in a thermal. Kingfishers, clustering on branches, preened their brilliant pink and blue feathers. An animal—an otter, was it?—briefly surfaced close to the boat, before plunging down again beneath the brown, swirling water.

It seemed impossible that this same, stately, flower-decked forest could have seemed so alien and menacing just a few short hours ago!

Despite the beauty of the morning, Hanna found it impossible to relax. Her sleep had been shallow, filled with wild dreams of strange-looking men clutching bottles of bright red blood.

Did the *bali saleng* really exist? Back home the whole thing would have seemed preposterous—crazy, even. But not here. People were extremely superstitious in this part of the world, even top businessmen and politicians. She could well believe they would be prepared to pay huge sums of money for blood if they thought it would guarantee success for their projects.

One thing was certain, though: the *bali saleng* were not demons, they were real people. They were murderous criminals trying to make a quick buck. Dodi had virtually admitted as much.

If he was right, somewhere in this forest—maybe not so far from where they were right now—lurked the *bali saleng* who'd murdered Felix. Their task was to find him and bring him to justice before Dad was executed for the brutal crime this loathsome creature had committed!

She glanced at the detective. He was sprawled against the side of the boat with his eyes closed. Now that she'd spotted it, it was impossible not to stare at his strange curved fingernail. She'd told the boys about it, and she saw that they couldn't keep their eyes off it either. It was a mystery why they hadn't noticed it earlier. None of the other men had one—she'd checked their hands while they were packing up camp that morning.

What did the claw mean, she wondered? Was it some sort of decoration, like a tattoo? Or did it mean something more sinister?

One thing she was sure of though—Ned's suggestion that Dodi had grown it specially to pick his nose couldn't possibly be right!

Towards mid-morning they hit more rapids—
even steeper than the ones back on the Kerai. They
just managed to scrape through. The water level
was very low, Pak Mulut told them, and there were
many dangerous stretches ahead. They would
have real problems reaching the upstream villages. When Jik asked him how far these villages
were, he spread his arms wide. 'Many kilometres!
Before that it is just forest—big, big forest.'

Unusually, the boat owner joined the children
when they stopped to eat at noon, squatting with
them in the shade of a fig tree at the side of the
river. It was the heat perhaps, but neither Hanna,
Ned, nor Jik felt hungry.

Pak Mulut became concerned. 'You must eat,'
he said urgently. 'It is important. You need
strength!'

'We've got strength,' Ned told him.

He shook his head. 'You need more! Eat now!'

Puzzled, they did what they were told.

The boat owner was certainly right about what
lay ahead. As soon as they had re-started their
journey, the sides of the river closed in and the
white water began. Soon the children were
drenched with spray, their bodies flung painfully
from side to side as the wild current threatened to
smash the *Maidah* to matchwood. Any moment, it
seemed, they would tip over, and be hurled to their

deaths in the raging torrent. Only Pak Mulut's skill, and the instant response of his four sons manning the engines, kept them safe.

It was all the more surprising then, when mid-way through the afternoon, on a calm bend of the river, the boat jerked to a sudden halt.

'What's happening?' Hanna asked, puzzled.

'Stuck!' was Dodi's terse reply. He was scanning the forest on either side of the river, as if trying to spot something—a landmark maybe. After a while he turned to the children. 'The water is too shallow. We must make the boat lighter. You must get out.' He pointed at some nearby rocks. 'Go, wait there.'

They lowered themselves into the water. It was surprisingly deep. Unless the boat was securely wedged, it ought to come free quite easily, Hanna thought, as they waded ashore.

The crew had jumped overboard too. They put their backs against the *Maidah*'s side and heaved.

It floated clear almost immediately.

The children hurried back towards it, expecting to be called on board; but they were ignored. The crew continued to push. Caught by the current, the boat suddenly swung completely round and pointed downstream in the direction they had come. The men threw themselves swiftly into it, and the engines roared into life. The *Maidah* sped away behind a spur of rock, and was lost from view.

Hanna, Ned, and Jik stood frozen to the spot, unable to believe their eyes. It had happened so quickly they didn't even have time to call out.

'What's going on?' Ned asked, in a stunned voice.

'I don't know! They've probably stopped nearby.' Hanna pointed at the rocky spur. 'We'll see them from up there.'

They scrambled up it. They spotted the *Maidah* immediately.

But it hadn't stopped.

It was speeding downstream. As they watched, it rounded a distant bend, and was gone.

Hanna felt numb with shock. 'It was deliberate,' she said in an unsteady voice. 'We've been deliberately dumped here!'

'But I don't understand,' Jik said. 'Why bring us all the way into the middle of goddam Borneo and then leave us here?'

'I don't know!' Hanna replied, panic setting in. 'There must be a reason, but I don't know it.'

She peered at the spot where the boat had disappeared, willing it to come back. But the river remained deserted. Apart from the chocolate-brown water, nothing moved. The only sounds were the rasping of cicadas and the buzz of small flies.

Ned tried to make the best of it. 'There'll be another boat come along soon, I expect,' he said brightly. 'Pak Mulut said there are villages upstream. The people who live there are bound to have boats. There'll be one along any minute.'

Jik wasn't so optimistic. 'How many other dam boats have we seen today?' he demanded.

'None,' Ned admitted. 'But it doesn't mean there won't be any. We just don't happen to have seen one.'

'Ned's right,' Hanna said. 'We must stay here and wait. Somebody's bound to come along sooner or later.'

It was hot on the rocks, and getting hotter by the minute. There was a broad-leaved tree growing close to the river's edge. They climbed shakily down and picked their way along the riverbank towards its welcoming shade.

Being out of the sun was such a relief! They sat down on a boulder and stared out at the river.

Even in her worst moments Hanna had never anticipated anything like this. It was clearly no accident. They hadn't been left here by chance. The whole thing must have been planned by Dodi right from the start—right from the moment he'd first met them in that back alley in Sangabera. It was as if they'd been *delivered* here, like one of Pak Mulut's sacks of rice.

But why?

And for whom?

The questions repeated themselves over and over in her brain.

Her thoughts were interrupted by Ned. 'I'm thirsty,' he complained.

'There's nothing to drink,' she told him.

'There's the river.'

'If you drink that water you'll get ill. It needs to be boiled.'

'If we don't drink anything we won't just get ill, we'll die.'

What he said was true. Hanna glanced up through the branches at the sky. It was a deep, tropical blue. She'd been hoping to see storm clouds building. But even if it did rain, they had nothing to collect the water in, she realized.

She thought back to when they'd been marooned on Shark Island after Mum and Dad had been captured by pirates. At least they'd had *some* things to help them survive there—fish-hooks; a saucepan to boil water; a box of matches to light a fire with. Here, they had nothing. Jik didn't even have his trusty knife—he'd been made to leave it at home in England when they'd set out.

Was that why Pak Mulut had urged them to eat all their food at lunchtime? Did he *know* they were going to be abandoned?

As the afternoon wore on, their thirst increased. Soon it became unbearable. Eventually Jik got to his feet. 'I go find dam water,' he said. 'Maybe there is a little stream close by.'

Ned offered to join him, and Hanna, not wanting to be left alone, announced that she would come too. After all, she reasoned, as long as they stayed close to the river they would hear any approaching boat long before it reached them, giving them plenty of time to get down to the shore and signal to it to stop.

They didn't find water, but they did find a path.

It was surprisingly wide, leading straight up the valley side from the riverbank, close to the spot where they'd been abandoned. There were no villages nearby, Hanna remembered Pak Mulut saying, so it must have been made by animals coming down to the river to drink.

They were climbing up it, wondering where it led to, when they heard a distant sound.

It was an engine!

'Quick!' Ned yelled, turning and leaping back down to the water's edge. Jik and Hanna rushed to join him.

A small motorized canoe was weaving downstream. It was empty apart from its driver, a thin, white-haired man. A fishing net was bunched in its bow.

The children jumped up and down, waving their arms, desperately trying to make themselves heard above the noise of the boat's engine. *'Stop!'* they yelled. *'Please stop!'*

The fisherman's look of surprise was clearly visible from across the water. He glanced round quickly, as if to check that they were alone, then he turned the canoe towards them. 'He's coming this way!' Jik exclaimed.

The boat nosed in to the bank at their feet and the engine cut. 'Tell him we need help!' Hanna said urgently. 'Tell him we've been abandoned here! Tell him we're dying of thirst!'

'Tolong kami . . . ' Jik began.

He didn't finish.

Echoing across the river came a scream.

It was even louder, even more blood-curdling than the one they'd heard the night before.

The effect on the fisherman was instant. His eyes widened in terror. He shoved his canoe back into the river, leapt into it, started the engine and shot away downstream.

'Don't leave us here!' Hanna yelled, rushing into the water after him.

Ned hauled her back. He was pointing across the river with a trembling finger.

Emerging from the jungle on the far bank was a man.

He was tall, brown-skinned, and was naked apart from a red loincloth wrapped round his waist. He was wearing a headdress of hornbill feathers like the ones the children had seen in Pak Mulut's house, and was clutching a long, sharp-pointed spear. A curved knife hung from his waist.

'It's the blood collector,' Ned gasped. 'It's the *bali saleng*!'

'Of course it's not!' Hanna snapped, deeply rattled. 'It's just somebody out for a walk!'

'Dressed like that? He's a Kenyah warrior. Dodi said a Kenyah warrior was the favourite form for a *bali saleng* to take!'

The man stopped at the edge of the river. He stared intently at the children. Then he opened his mouth and screamed again.

It was the scream of a ruthless predator sighting its prey.

There was a set of rapids close to where he was standing. Using his spear as a vaulting pole, he leapt across, covering huge distances from rock to rock. Moments later he was on their side of the river, and running swiftly down the bank towards them. As he got closer, they could see his face. It was deeply-lined; cruel.

Suddenly Hanna understood. They'd been brought here to become victims of this evil creature! He was going to slaughter them, drain their blood, sell it for huge sums of money. Dodi must be in on the act, taking a cut. Pak Mulut too. 'Let's get out of here!' she yelled to the boys.

There was only one possible escape route—up the path they'd just discovered. The rest of the riverbank was covered with impenetrable, thorny undergrowth. They turned and sprinted towards it—Jik in the lead, followed by Ned, with Hanna a close third.

The path was steep and slippery. The children grabbed at rocks and vines to haul themselves upwards. Progress was terrifyingly slow.

Yet another scream. The *bali saleng* had reached the bottom of the path and was scrambling quickly up after them. His legs were long and wiry. He was catching up fast. If only there was some way of stopping him!

The path grew even steeper. The thump of the man's footsteps was getting louder by the second. Hanna's heart sank. Any moment now he would reach out and grab her . . .

He didn't.

Puzzled, she glanced back over her shoulder.

He'd slowed, and seemed to be deliberately keeping pace with them, a few metres behind.

After a while the path levelled out. The going was easier now, and the children picked up speed, sprinting for their lives, their lungs bursting. But the man stayed with them, matching them step for step.

Were they being *driven* somewhere—like sheep?

The thought had hardly occurred to Hanna when a sudden shout of terror rang out. The floor of the path had given way, and Ned and Jik had plunged headlong through it.

Unable to stop herself in time, she crashed down on top of them.

9

The Pit

Gasping for breath, spitting out leaves and twigs, the children untangled themselves. Miraculously, nobody seemed to be hurt. The pit was deep, and had been expertly dug, its sides sloping inwards. There was no way they could get out without help.

Not that they wanted to at that precise moment.

Their pursuer was staring down at them with bloodshot eyes. He wore a triumphant smile, his lips drawn back to reveal a set of gold-capped teeth. 'What do you want with us?' Hanna asked, her voice faint with terror.

The only reply was a monosyllabic grunt.

Jik tried repeating the question in Indonesian. The response was the same.

The man disappeared. Soon afterwards, he returned. He was carrying a crude ladder made from lashed-together lengths of bamboo. He lowered it into the pit.

The children cowered back against the crumbling earth walls.

The man pointed at Hanna and made another loud grunting sound. He was saying something. It was '*Girl*', she suddenly realized.

Never had such a familiar word sounded so terrifying.

He was indicating that she should climb the ladder.

Ned grabbed her arm. 'Stay here!' he hissed frantically. 'If you go up there we'll have no chance. We must make him come down to us. Then we can all fight him!'

'I dam kill him!' Jik exploded. 'I dam kill him with my bare hands!'

'*Girl!*'

The man's smile had disappeared. He was getting angry.

'*GIRL!*'

It was not so much a grunt now, as a roar.

'Come down here and get us!' Ned yelled up at him, blind fury overcoming his terror. 'Or are you too much of a coward?'

There was no response. The man had gone.

Moments later he was back, clutching his spear. With a furious bellow, he flung it at Ned.

It missed him by millimetres.

The man pulled it up and hurled it again. This time it grazed Hanna's arm, before burying itself into the floor at her feet.

It seemed impossible that they hadn't been hit. Was the man *toying* with them?

Jik was the target now—but he was ready for it. As the spear hurtled down at him, he leapt sideways and grabbed its shaft. 'Help me!' he yelled desperately to the others.

Ned and Hanna flung themselves across the pit and added their grip to his. If they were strong enough they might even manage to pull their attacker down on top of them.

But the spear was slippery. Despite their best efforts they couldn't stop it sliding back through their fingers. 'Let go!' Ned yelled at the last minute, as its razor-sharp blade threatened to slice their hands in two.

It was hopeless. Any moment now, one of them was going to get killed—or badly hurt. 'Stop it! I'm coming up!' Hanna yelled, tears of frustration and rage clouding her eyes.

She broke away from the boys, and scrambled up the ladder. Ned's desperate shouts rose up after her.

The man reached down and jerked her roughly onto the path. The ladder was pulled up immediately after her, trapping Ned and Jik below. 'Take my blood!' Hanna screamed at him. 'I've got plenty of blood! You can have all of it. But let the boys go. They're only young. They're . . . '

A fist cracked against the side of her head. 'Silence!' the man snarled. 'Put on!'

He was pointing at something.

Hanna struggled to focus. There was what looked like a heap of rusty metal lying at the base of a tree. She was dragged towards it.

They were leg irons, she realized, like large handcuffs. She remembered seeing pictures of them when she'd done a slavery project at school. They were locked round people's ankles to stop them running away.

A kick sent her sprawling. *'Put on!'*

With trembling hands she pulled a pair from the heap. There were three pairs in all, joined to each other by a length of chain.

The irons were tight, cutting into her ankles. The man reached down and locked them into place. 'Stay!' he ordered.

It was as if he was talking to a dog.

He returned to the pit, lowered the ladder. Jik was the next up, protesting loudly until silenced by a vicious blow. He too was locked into the leg irons.

Then, finally, it was Ned's turn.

When all three of them were secured the man disappeared behind a tree. To the children's astonishment he emerged a short while later wearing a modern army uniform, and carrying a semi-automatic rifle. What on earth was going on?

He hauled the children to their feet. 'We go!' he said, in a hard voice, pointing along the path.

As he did so, Hanna noticed that one fingernail on his left hand was curved into the shape of a claw.

Being chained together made walking seriously difficult. Several times they tripped and fell. Hanna led the way, followed by Jik, with Ned at the rear. She could feel the blood beginning to flow as the sharp metal bit into the soft flesh of her ankles.

The path led away from the river, deep into the forest. Despite the shade, the heat and humidity was intense. Hanna's thirst returned, much worse than before. Glancing back, she could see that the boys were in trouble too. They had to have water soon or they would collapse. She tried to tell their captor, but all she received was another blow.

The trek seemed to go on for ever. They discovered that walking was easier if they held on to each other's shoulders, and kept in step like marching soldiers. The man seemed to find this amusing, and marched beside them making exaggerated movements with his arms and legs as they clanked along. Hanna wondered when he would call a halt and the bloodletting would begin.

Then, unexpectedly, the path broadened out and the trees thinned. Ahead of them was what looked like a long rectangular meadow. The grass had been mown recently, and its surface was smooth and level.

It was a jungle airstrip—where small planes could land and take off.

Facing on to it was an open-fronted thatched hut. The children were pushed inside, made to sit down, then chained to one of the stout posts that supported its roof.

Their captor unclipped a small, hand-held radio from a holster on his belt, and began to talk into it in Indonesian. He made no attempt to hide what he was saying. 'He is calling his boss,' Jik whispered to Hanna and Ned. 'He is saying that everything has gone to plan, and to send the plane for us as soon as dam possible.'

'Where are we being taken to?' Ned asked.

Jik shook his head. 'I don't know. He hasn't said.'

The man was making exasperated noises, clearly unhappy about something. 'They say that the plane cannot get here until tomorrow morning,' Jik explained. 'Something is wrong with its engine. It makes him dam mad.'

The man switched off his radio with an angry click, and shoved it back into its holster. There was a cardboard box in a corner of the hut. Muttering to himself he went to it and took out a large bottle of drinking water. He drained it in a series of loud gulps, belched loudly, and threw the empty bottle back into the box.

The sight of the water was almost too much for the children to bear. 'Please!' Hanna begged desperately. 'We need to drink!'

Their captor ignored her, picked up his gun and went to the door of the hut. He stared up into the evening sky as if willing a plane to appear by magic.

Jik tried Indonesian. *'Minum!'* he croaked, pointing at his mouth. *'Mahu minum!'*

'If we don't get water we're going to die!' Ned chimed in.

At last the man got the message. He sighed irritably, and went to the box. He took out a fresh bottle of water and threw it at the children.

They drank it greedily. Feeling much better, they looked around.

The hut was empty, apart from the cardboard box, which hopefully contained more bottles of water. Their captor must have brought it with him when he'd arrived—presumably by plane.

What puzzled Hanna was *why*?

Why go to the trouble and expense of clearing an airstrip and paying for a plane to fly into it, just to capture three children and steal their blood? However much it was worth, it surely didn't justify this. Come to that, why hadn't their captor just cut their throats and collected their blood back there in the jungle? He could have done it easily, and disposed of their bodies without any problem.

Unless—and the very thought made her shiver—*unless* the blood he collected had to come from a *living* person! Were they being taken somewhere to become *human sacrifices*? It was the only answer she could think of.

She was about to share her thoughts with the boys when she stopped herself. There were some things it was best not to tell them.

Somehow they had to escape! But how on earth could they do it when they were chained up like dogs? Short of getting hold of the keys which their captor kept in the top pocket of his uniform, they would need heavy cutting gear to get themselves free.

The sun was setting. The man ate a packet of instant noodles, which he crunched up like crisps without boiling them. Then he went outside to smoke cigarettes. It was clear that only he was going to get food that night.

Trying to ignore their hunger, the children shifted to get more comfortable. As they did so, there was an exclamation from Ned. 'Look at this!' he said excitedly.

He was pointing at the wooden wall behind

him. Scratched into it was the name FELIX. Beneath it was a date six weeks earlier.

'He was here!' Jik said. 'Felix was here, chained up just like us!'

Hanna felt a shiver run through her. This was the first piece of proper evidence they'd found! Felix must have been captured at the gold workings and brought to this hut. He'd obviously spent some time chained to this very post—long enough to scratch his name on the wall—before presumably being loaded onto a plane and flown to his death.

One thing was sickeningly clear: whoever their captor was, he, and the people he was working for, were directly involved in Felix's murder.

And the same fate was almost certainly in store for them.

10

Sweet Revenge

Darkness fell, and the moon rose, giving off a bright silvery light. After a final cigarette, their captor came back inside the hut and settled down to sleep opposite the children, using the small backpack he'd been wearing as a pillow. His gun was next to him.

Hanna, Jik, and Ned stayed awake for a long time, the pain from their ankles, squeezed by the heavy leg-irons, making sleep virtually impossible. Outside, nightjars shrieked, and bats swooped and fluttered.

Eventually, Hanna fell into a light doze, her sleep punctuated by vivid and violent dreams. In one of them, an old witch was jabbing a red-hot needle into her thigh.

She tried to escape from her, but couldn't.

The needle pierced her again, and again.

Her eyes flicked open. Though the dream had gone, the pain remained. Suddenly she understood why: something very nasty had bitten her.

A sudden yelp from Ned told her that he, too, was under attack.

It was ants! Hanna could see them in the moonlight, scurrying in through the open front of the hut. They were heading towards Jik. A rustling noise, followed by a baby-like sucking sound revealed why.

He'd taken a small sachet of sugar out of his pocket—the kind you get in restaurants with your tea or coffee—and was pouring it down his throat. He adored sugar, and despite everything Mum told him about it rotting his teeth, he always collected loads of it when he got the chance.

He must have grabbed a handful at the hotel back in Sangabera, and had kept it with him all this time.

There was just one problem: the inhabitants of a nearby ant colony had scented the sweetness, and were scurrying to get their share. Judging by their stings, they were fire ants—the most vicious and painful ants of all.

'Get rid of that stuff!' Hanna hissed angrily.

Jik, who was now being bitten himself, needed no second bidding. He got to his knees, ready to throw the offending packet outside.

Ned stopped him. 'Wait!' he whispered excitedly. 'I've just had a crazy idea. It might work. Have you got any more of that sugar?'

Jik nodded. He sheepishly reached into his pocket and took out another half-dozen sachets. They were wrapped in plastic to keep them dry.

'Brilliant! Here's the plan.'

Ned breathed it into Jik's ear. The Sea Gypsy boy's face broke into a broad smile.

'What are you going to do?' Hanna whispered.

'You'll see!'

Moving slowly, to prevent their chains rattling, the two boys squirmed as close as they could to their captor. Judging by his loud snores, he was still sound asleep. They ripped the tops off the sugar sachets and scattered the contents over his face and body. He snorted, shifted slightly, but didn't wake up. Soon he looked like a birthday cake dusted with icing!

The boys quickly returned to their positions next to Hanna, and sat back to watch.

There were lots more ants now—countless thousands of them—advancing on the hut like a miniature invading army. At the entrance to the building they paused in the moonlight, rearing up on their back legs, feelers waving, as they scented the delicious sweetness inside.

Then, locking on to its source, they hurried towards it.

Within seconds the sleeping man was a seething mass of insects, with hundreds more crawling under his shirt and up his trouser legs, hunting for the scattered grains.

For a short while he slept on.

Then the first sting pierced his skin.

Irritably, he slapped at the spot, killing a dozen ants in the process.

The scent of death joined the scent of sugar. It was the trigger for a massive attack. Instantly, he was being stung all over his body by countless furious insects.

Bellowing with pain, he leapt to his feet, ripped off his clothes, and wearing only his underpants, charged outside.

Now Hanna understood. This was exactly what the boys had hoped would happen! The man's shirt had landed on the floor close to her. Braving the angry ants, she grabbed it and took out the keys.

With trembling hands, she unlocked their shackles. It seemed to take an age as she searched for the right key for each lock; but eventually she managed it.

They were free!

Their captor's gun was lying on the floor next to his backpack. Ned grabbed it and followed Jik and Hanna outside into the bright moonlight.

They were met by an extraordinary sight. The man was in the centre of the airstrip, performing a weird, jerky dance; alternatively slapping at his bare skin, then rolling on the ground to try to rub off the ants he couldn't reach. As they got closer they could see there were insects in his hair too, and in his ears. He was howling with pain. Hanna almost felt sorry for him.

Almost . . .

Suddenly, the truth dawned. Thanks to Ned's brilliant idea, they'd not only managed to get themselves free, but they'd got his gun too. He was completely in their power.

Now, surely, they'd be able to get the answers to some very important questions.

They raced up to him, Ned with the gun levelled. The man was no longer dancing, but had slumped to the ground. He was in a bad way, his face and body swelling rapidly as the poison took hold.

'Ask him if he killed Felix,' Hanna said.

Jik put the question.

There was no reply.

Ned rammed the gun into the man's back. 'Answer us!'

This time there was a slurred response.

Jik translated with difficulty: 'He says he didn't kill the German. He was taken away in an aeroplane.'

'Where to?'

'The Arena.'

'Where's that?'

'He says please can you get the ants off him.'

Hanna's jaw tightened. 'Only if he answers our questions!'

The man muttered something incomprehensible. Losing patience, Ned bellowed into his ears as if he was deaf: 'Tell us where this Arena place is!'

There was no answer. The man's head had slumped forwards. He was unconscious.

Furious, Hanna brushed as many of the ants off him as she could, and slapped his cheeks. 'Wake up!' she yelled. 'We've got questions to ask you. Lots of questions!'

His eyes remained shut.

'Do you think he's going to die?' Jik asked.

'I don't know,' Hanna replied. 'He probably needs antihistamines or something. Some people are allergic to insect stings.'

'Well, he's out of luck,' Ned said, as disappointed as his sister.

'We put water on him?' Jik suggested.

'We don't have any water, except in that box, and we mustn't waste that,' Hanna said.

'So what?'

'I don't know.' She glanced around. Beyond the airstrip the jungle loomed, dark and menacing. They might have got themselves free, but they were not much closer to the truth. And time was running out.

They dragged the unconscious man none too gently to the nearest tree, and using their leg irons, chained him to it. Then, after making sure there were no more angry ants around, they sat down to discuss what to do next.

Unless the man regained consciousness, how on earth could they possibly find out where this mysterious Arena was? It could be a thousand miles away, and they had no idea in which direction it lay.

But somehow they had to get there.

They tried desperately to come up with an answer. A large white beetle, the size of a ping-pong ball, droned towards them and crash-landed at their feet. They were watching its struggle to get airborne again when Ned suddenly let out a loud exclamation: 'Yes!'

'Yes what?' Hanna demanded.

His eyes flashed with excitement. 'That beetle thing's just given me an idea! We fly there!'

'We fly?'

'Remember what that man said on his radio? A plane's coming to collect us tomorrow morning. All we need to do is get on board it and it'll take us straight to this Arena place!'

Hanna and Jik stared at Ned open mouthed.

'But we've only just dam escaped!' Jik exclaimed. 'You want us to give ourselves up again? We'll get killed—like Felix!'

Ned shook his head. 'Not if we're clever. Remember, we've got a gun now. We can use it to capture the pilot when he arrives. Then we make him fly us there, but not land. We take a note of its exact position—there's bound to be a GPS on board—then head for the nearest big city and tell the police.'

'It won't work,' Hanna put in. 'Even if the plane's got enough fuel to take us all that way, we'll be arrested for hijacking the moment we land—and I know whose story the police will believe. We'll get locked up like Mum and Dad and probably never get let out.'

'How about we make the pilot land us close to the Arena,' Jik suggested. 'Then we tie him up and sneak through the jungle until we reach it. Once it's dark, we can slip inside and search for clues. I bet we'll find trillions straight away. Easy dam peasy.'

It didn't sound easy to Hanna. Or particularly dam peasy. It sounded seriously dangerous. And how would they get away afterwards? Nobody had even thought about that. But what alternative did they have? From now on, it was all or nothing.

Jik would handle the gun, they decided, and

Hanna and Ned would act as decoys. There was a patch of tall elephant grass midway along the airstrip. Jik would conceal himself in there, while Hanna and Ned stood next to it and attracted the attention of the pilot when he landed. When he came across to investigate, Jik would rise up out of the grass, and capture him. Then they'd all get into the plane and take off.

As they waited for dawn, Hanna felt a dull dread. It seemed such a desperate, foolhardy thing to attempt! So much could go wrong.

She reached for the string in her pocket, and untied a knot to signal the beginning of a new day. There were only twenty-one knots left now—just three weeks to find the evidence they needed.

Time was passing so quickly!

She wondered how Mum and Dad were getting on. Dad must be feeling so desperate and lonely in his horrible prison cell. She wanted to go to him, hug him, tell him everything would be all right—that she and Ned and Jik wouldn't stop for one single second until they'd got him free.

Jik had taken the gun from Ned and was examining it closely in the moonlight. It looked different from some of the other weapons they'd seen—smaller, lighter. It was almost as if something was missing from it. It was stamped 'Tentera Nasional' which meant it was army property.

Hanna glanced across at the man, who was still slumped unconscious against the tree. She had assumed his army uniform was as fake as the loin-cloth and feathers he'd been wearing when they'd first seen him.

Obviously not.

Judging by his gun he was a genuine soldier. That meant that whatever was going on here involved the army—or at least some of it—and he'd been following orders. Far from becoming clearer, things were getting more puzzling by the minute.

11

Hijack

They heard the aircraft before they saw it, the drone of its engine cutting through the chorus of monkey hoots and birdsong that greeted the new day. Jik grabbed the gun and leapt into the elephant grass, pulling the fronds down on top of him. Hanna just had time to check that he was properly hidden, before the plane came into view. It was a small, single-engined machine, painted a dull green to match the colour of the jungle. There were no identity numbers on its fuselage or wings.

It circled the airstrip, then came in to land, bouncing twice on the uneven surface, before coming to a halt. Immediately, it swung round and taxied across to where Hanna and Ned were standing. Its engine cut, the cockpit door was flung open, and the pilot jumped out.

To their surprise, he was a white man—quite young, with fair hair and piercing blue eyes. 'What's going on here?' he demanded, peering round. 'Where's Baya?' Judging by his accent he was American.

'Who's Baya?' Hanna asked, desperate to gain and keep his attention.

'The soldier man. The dude who's meant to be bringing you in.'

Hanna became aware of Jik rising silently out of the grass behind him. She prayed that Ned wouldn't give the game away by glancing in his direction.

He didn't.

'Baya's sick,' she said. 'He got stung by ants . . . '

The pilot's eyes widened in alarm as he felt the barrel of Jik's gun press into his back.

Ned began to speak smoothly, as if his words had been carefully rehearsed. 'Don't turn round, but there's a rifle pointed straight at your spine. My friend will use it if you make one false move. And don't think that just because he's a kid he won't pull the trigger.'

'He means what he says,' Hanna snarled, trying to sound fierce. 'Put your hands up!'

The pilot slowly raised his arms. *As he did so, she saw that he too, had a claw on his left hand.*

The boys had spotted it as well. It seemed to make them even more determined. 'Now turn round slowly and walk back to your goddam plane!' Jik ordered. 'And don't try to be clever!'

'OK, you're the boss.'

At the cockpit door the pilot stopped. 'What now?'

'We get in,' Ned told him. 'Then we take off and you fly us out of here.'

'Where to?'

'Where we tell you to!'

This was unreal, Hanna was thinking. It was like something out of a movie.

The pilot half-turned. For the first time he was able to see Jik clearly. His eyes flicked down to the gun. A slow smile spread across his face. 'So you're hijackers, hey? What if I refuse to be hijacked?'

'Then we shoot you!' Ned spat.

'I don't think you will.'

'Why not?'

The pilot's smile broadened. 'For two good reasons. First, if you shoot me you won't be going anywhere—unless one of you can fly a Cessna 185, which I very much doubt. Second, your friend's rifle doesn't have a magazine fitted, so he can't shoot anybody, even if he wanted to.'

Hanna peered at the gun. Her heart sank. The magazine that held the bullets was missing. That was why the weapon had seemed different! How could they have been so stupid?

The pilot reached into the plane and took out a pistol. He waved it in the direction of the children. 'On the other hand, this little fella *is* loaded and I know how to use it. I wouldn't want you to get hurt. So why don't you three stay just exactly where you are while I call home?'

He climbed back into the cockpit and reached for the radio. As he did so, he spotted Baya in the distance, chained to his tree.

His attention was distracted for a moment.

A moment was all it took.

'Come on!' yelled Jik, throwing down the gun. 'Let's go!'

He turned and sprinted across the grass towards the jungle.

Hanna and Ned raced after him.

The trees were no more than fifty metres away, but it seemed like a million miles. Hanna urged herself onwards, waiting for the thud of a bullet into her back and the searing agony that would follow.

It didn't come.

There were shouts, shots. She glanced at the boys, expecting to see one or both of them fall; but like her, they seemed to be living a charmed life. Despite his boast, the pilot must have a very bad aim indeed.

They reached the forest, and plunged into the undergrowth. 'Keep going!' Ned yelled, as they fought their way through.

Hanna glanced back. The pilot had started to

chase them, but had stopped at the edge of the airstrip. He fired off two final shots, then turned and ran quickly back towards his plane. Its engine burst into life. It taxied to the end of the runway, and took off.

The further the children penetrated into the forest, the easier it became. Jik was in the lead now, speeding over a carpet of fallen leaves down the side of a shallow valley. It was surprisingly cool in the dense shade, and so dark you almost needed a torch to see where you were going.

They'd come a long way in a very short time, but even though their bodies were screaming at them to stop, the children kept on running. They could hear the drone of the plane's engine as it circled above the treetops. Twice they saw its silhouette through the spreading branches. The pilot was trying to spot them, Hanna guessed, trying to find out which way they were heading before calling for help.

After what seemed like an age, the noise of the engine began to fade, and then died away completely. Only then did they allow themselves to finally stop. They looked at each other triumphantly, their chests heaving.

They'd done it. They were safe!

But for how long?

12
Lost

The children sat down on a fallen log to rest, and pick the thorns from their blood-streaked arms and legs. As they did so, the sheer idiocy of what they'd just done struck Hanna with the force of a sledgehammer. 'Why on earth did you decide to run?' she said to Jik accusingly. 'It's a miracle we weren't all killed!'

He looked indignant. 'No dam miracle! That pilot was trying to make us stop—not dam kill us.'

'How do you know that?' Ned challenged.

'Because if not we would be dead already! The *bali saleng* man would have cut our throats back at the river. These people want to keep us alive for some dam reason. No way are they going to shoot us if they can help it.'

Jik had reached the same conclusion as she had, Hanna realized, and had taken a calculated gamble by trying to escape. She wondered again whether she should share her fears about *why* they were being kept alive with the boys, but decided against it.

There was little more to be said. When they'd got their breath back, Ned stood up. 'Let's get going. That plane will be back soon. They're bound to send trackers—people who can trace where we've gone. We'd better get as far away from here as possible before that happens.'

There was a hilly ridge to the east, back-lit by the rising sun. There might well be a river on the other side. Where there were rivers there were villages. Maybe they could find someone who could help them. They set off briskly towards it.

For the first couple of hours the going was easy. It was like walking through a huge cathedral. Massive buttressed tree trunks soared skywards, their lowest branches at least thirty metres above the children's heads. Between them were scores of small saplings, pushing hopefully upwards towards the distant canopy. Except where a tree had fallen to allow light in, there was very little undergrowth, and no noise apart from the constant buzz and hum of insects. Though Hanna knew she was being watched by scores of hidden eyes, she felt strangely alone, and wondered if the boys felt the same.

After a while the ground began to rise sharply. Jik took over at the front. Ned looked pale and exhausted, Hanna saw, as she caught up with him. It was hunger, she supposed. They'd eaten nothing for almost twenty-four hours. They had to find food and water soon—but where?

It was Jik who spotted the fruit tree—or rather, spotted the monkeys who had found it first. There was a large troop of them, crashing and squabbling in the upper branches of a broad-leaved giant, showering half-eaten fruit down onto the forest floor below.

Jik picked one up and handed it to Hanna. It was bright orange, and looked a bit like a shrivelled-up apple. Should they—*could* they—eat it?

Hanna asked Jik, but he didn't know. During their adventures in the islands he could always tell what was edible and what was not. But here in the jungle, he was as unsure as she was.

She peered up through the branches. The monkeys were certainly tucking into the fruit with gusto. They were our nearest relatives, she knew. Presumably that meant that what they could eat, we could eat too. It was worth the risk, she decided.

After checking there was no monkey-dribble on the fruit that Jik had given her, she took an experimental bite.

Far from tasting horrible, as she'd expected, it tasted of . . . nothing at all. It was soft and pulpy— a bit like eating mashed potato.

But it was food. Like the monkeys, she realized,

if you were going to survive you had to eat what you found.

The fruit made Jik and Hanna feel better—but not much. Ned didn't finish the one he was given.

After a brief rest, they continued onwards. The slope steepened further, until they were climbing almost vertically. Strange bulbous outcrops of rock began to occur. Suddenly Jik stopped and pointed at one of them. A long time ago—centuries probably—it had been carved into a weird scowling face. Was it meant to be a frog or a human? It was impossible to tell.

Hanna showed it to Ned. Normally he loved ancient things like this, and wanted to know everything about the people who'd made them. But today he didn't seem to be interested. When she asked him if he felt OK, he nodded, but didn't reply.

It got darker as they climbed. Close to the top of the ridge, Jik paused, sniffed the air. 'Rain come soon,' he declared.

He was right. Minutes later the heavens opened. There was no warning—no thunder or lightning—just water suddenly cascading from the sky onto their heads. It was as if a massive fire-hose had been turned on.

Within seconds the track they'd been following turned into a gushing waterfall. It became impossible to climb—impossible to even see. Gasping for

breath in the deluge, the children pressed themselves against the trunk of a nearby tree.

It gave them some shelter—but not much. As
the deluge increased, loud cracks and crashes
began to echo through the jungle. For a while
Hanna was puzzled; but then she realized it must
be huge branches, weighed down by the mass of
ferns and moss clinging to them, snapping off the
trees and plummeting down to the forest floor
below.

She peered upwards fearfully. Would the same
thing happen to a branch on their tree? Maybe
they should find an open space where they were
less likely to get crushed. Maybe . . .

Maybe they should do a lot of things . . .

As the rainwater hammered at her head, for the
first time she began to understand the deadly danger they were in. They were completely helpless—
at the mercy of whatever the jungle might throw at
them.

The rain stopped eventually, and the sun came
out, strewing the forest floor with twinkling, dia-
mond-shaped points of light. As the heat
increased, the air became heavy with water
vapour. Sweating from every pore, scarcely able to
breathe, the children hauled themselves onwards
and upwards. There were only a few hours left
before darkness fell—only a few hours to find the

food and shelter that could make the difference between life and death.

'Leech!'

It was Jik who spotted one first. It had attached itself to his thigh. It was browny-black, as thick as a slug after gorging itself on his blood.

Then Hanna found one too. It had wriggled up under her shirt and pierced her skin near her tummy button. Amazingly, she felt no pain. That was because leeches injected an anaesthetic with their bite, she knew; but it didn't make having your blood sucked any more pleasant.

Suddenly there were leeches everywhere. Ned had two on his neck, and several more on his arms and legs. Hundreds of others were hanging upside down from nearby leaves, stretching out their wormlike bodies towards the children as they scented fresh blood; or looping rapidly along twigs and branches, trying to get close enough to spring onto them as they passed.

As more and more of them attached themselves to him, Ned's usual bravery deserted him. 'Get them off me!' he yelled frantically at Hanna. 'I don't like these things!'

The leeches were very hard to remove—firmly attached by their sharp teeth, unwilling to let go until their feast was complete. They had to be pinched clear, then flicked quickly away before they could lock themselves on again.

They'd injected an anti-coagulant along with the anaesthetic, which meant that the blood kept flowing long after they'd been pinched off. Soon the children looked as if they'd been the victims of a nasty road accident.

Eventually they managed to get rid of most of them, and they set off again, still aiming to cross the ridge. The going was much more difficult now, the path slippery with mud. Hanna stayed close to her brother, helping him past the difficult bits, encouraging him with jokes and comments. She was increasingly worried about him. He seemed to be getting weaker with every step.

After an hour or so, Jik suddenly stopped. 'Look!' he said, in an anguished voice.

Hanna peered through the leaves at where he was pointing. Ahead of them was a large rounded rock, carved into the shape of a face.

It was the same rock they'd seen earlier.

Without realizing it, they'd walked in a huge circle and arrived back at where they'd started.

13

Fever

Ned sank to the ground. 'I can't walk any further,' he gasped.

Hanna put out a hand to comfort him.

His skin felt burning hot.

He had a fever, she realized. A bad one! Was it malaria—or something worse? Whatever it was, he needed treatment fast.

When she told Jik, his face creased with worry. 'We must go back to the airstrip,' he said. 'Maybe that pilot has medicine in his dam plane.'

'The plane's gone.'

'It'll come back.'

Hanna contemplated her brother, slumped at the side of the path, small insects sucking at the dribbles of saliva oozing from his lips. 'He'll never be able to walk that far,' she said.

'We make stretcher.'

'We've got nothing to make it with.'

Jik took a deep breath. 'OK, I carry him then! I carry him on my dam back! He can't stay in this place.'

He bent, helped his friend to his feet. Ned muttered something about being able to walk on his own, but his protests were ignored. With Hanna's help he was hoisted onto Jik's back.

He was quite heavy, and Jik could only just lift him. Swaying unsteadily the two boys set off down the narrow track they'd just climbed up. Hanna followed close behind.

Could they really find their way back to the airstrip? She doubted it strongly. And even if they could, what guarantee was there that they'd be given any help? She tried to spot landmarks—familiar-looking trees or bushes. But everywhere seemed the same—a soggy mass of insect-infested greenery. Soon it was clear that they were once again completely lost.

Jik staggered on for an incredible length of time. But then, on a muddy slope, he lost his footing, and the two boys crashed into an untidy heap. Hanna hurried up to them.

The Sea Gypsy boy was gasping for breath, soaked with sweat and mud. He was close to his limit, she saw. 'I'll take over,' she told him.

'I rest! I be OK in a dam minute.'

'You're being stupid. It's my turn!'

Hanna managed maybe five hundred metres with Ned on her back, before she, too, could go no further. It was hopeless! They were miles from safety—even if they knew in which direction safety lay. As she crouched panting on the path, desperately trying to get her breath back, Jik put a finger to his lips. 'Listen,' he said.

Hanna listened. At first all she could hear was the usual cacophony of insect and frog noises. But then came a new sound.

Water.

Gushing water!

Jik leapt to his feet and disappeared through a screen of bushes. Seconds later he was back. 'It's a goddam river!' he said triumphantly. Helping Ned to his feet, they half-led, half-carried him towards it.

It wasn't so much a river as a tiny stream, gurgling between moss-covered rocks. Swarms of vivid blue and red dragonflies hovered over its surface. The water was clear and cool. Hanna washed her muddy hands, then scooped some up. It tasted clean and fresh—it was surely safe to drink.

They found a shady spot among the rocks and sat Ned down in it. Jik made a crude cup from a large leaf and filled it with water. Ned was reluctant to drink, but eventually managed to swallow a couple of mouthfuls, which he promptly vomited up. His face was bright red, flushed with fever. He was clearly very ill.

Hanna remembered Granny telling her about

how, when Grandpa had got ill on an army mission once, his comrades had bathed him with cold water to keep his temperature down until help had arrived. She must do the same for Ned!

She eased off his shirt, dunked it in the stream, and began to bathe him with it. 'Does that feel better?' she whispered.

Ned nodded weakly, his eyes closed. Soothed, he fell into a shallow sleep.

Hanna glanced up at Jik. 'You must go for help,' she said firmly. 'I'll stay here with Ned.'

Jik stared wildly round. 'But I don't know where to dam go!'

'Follow the stream. It'll join a bigger river eventually, where there'll be people. You've got brown skin so they won't think you're a *bali saleng*. They're bound to help!'

'But you've got no food!'

'People can last for days without food!' Hanna sounded much more confident than she felt.

The Sea Gypsy boy's eyes met hers. He looked so young and vulnerable in the fading light. He took a deep breath. 'OK. I go,' he announced, with new determination. 'And I come back dam soon!'

He wanted to set off straight away, but Hanna stopped him. Night was falling. Soon it would be impossible to see. Stumbling about in the darkness, he could break a leg—or worse. He'd start at dawn. It would be downhill all the way, so he'd make good progress. With any luck he could be back with help in two or three days.

Hanna glanced anxiously down at her brother. Without proper medical help could he last that long? Could he survive another *day*, let alone two or three? She bent and kissed his burning forehead. She loved him so much it hurt.

The night seemed to go on for ever. She and Jik took turns at bathing Ned, desperately trying to keep him cool. His bouts of high fever alternated with periods when he complained that he was cold, his whole body shaking violently. During those times, Hanna pressed herself against him to give him warmth. Towards the end of the night he became delirious, convinced he was being attacked by blood-sucking vampire bats. Jik had to pretend to shoot them before he calmed down enough to go to sleep again.

Dawn broke eventually, a pale green light filtering between the trees, giving the weird impression that they were somehow under water. It was like a prearranged signal. Instantly the jungle began to echo with the hoots and shouts of gibbons and orang-utans, invisible in the treetops. Every bird in Borneo seemed to join in, whistling and squawking and screeching at the tops of their voices.

Hanna, who had fallen asleep for a few minutes, wedged against her brother, woke up with a start. She reached out and felt his skin. It was still hot, but no longer burning. The constant bathing had obviously helped. He was asleep, his head flopped back like a dead person's.

She glanced across at Jik. He, too, was asleep, sprawled on a flat rock next to the stream, exhausted by the night's events, and the exertions of the day before. It seemed so cruel to wake him— but she knew she had no alternative. He had a long way to go, and if he was to have any chance of success an early start was essential.

She was about to call out to him, when a movement on the far bank of the stream caught her eye.

At first she thought it was a rat. But then the creature emerged from the shadows and she could see it more clearly. It was a deer—the smallest deer she'd ever seen. It had dark brown fur, spindly, sticklike legs, and stood no more than twenty centimetres high. With its big round eyes and shiny black nose, it reminded her of Bambi.

It had to be a mouse-deer—the smallest deer in the world! Hanna remembered Dad telling her about them. It glanced quickly round to check that all was well, and bent its head to drink.

At that instant, something extraordinary happened.

There was a soft 'phut' sound from behind a nearby rock, and the little deer suddenly leapt into the air. For a few seconds it struggled to get back into the undergrowth at the edge of the stream, but then its legs buckled beneath it, and it collapsed. It twitched several times, and was still. Sticking out of its side was what looked like a wooden knitting needle.

Hanna glanced around in panic. What on earth was going on?

Then a second movement caught her eye. Jumping from rock to rock across the stream was a small girl.

She was bare-footed, wearing a tattered, mud-coloured singlet and shorts. Her hair was cut into a straight fringe across her forehead. She was holding a long wooden spear. Following close on her heels were three small brown hunting dogs.

She reached the deer; examined it closely.

Then she stopped, and stared.

First at Jik, who was still sleeping; next at Ned sprawled amongst the rocks; finally at Hanna.

If the girl was surprised, she didn't show it. She spoke softly to the dogs, who were beginning to growl, and they fell silent. She bent down, removed the knitting needle from the deer's flank, and slipped it into a bamboo quiver hung from her waist. Then she leapt across the stream to where Hanna was sitting.

After a moment's silence, while the two girls contemplated each other, it was the newcomer who spoke first. 'What is your name?' she asked, in clear, accent-free English.

Astonished, Hanna told her.

'My name is Muni,' the girl said matter-of-factly, 'though Po calls me Mini because I am so extremely little. I'm very pleased to meet you.'

'I'm . . . er . . . very pleased to meet you too,' Hanna replied, not quite believing what she was seeing, or hearing.

'And these are my dogs—Bahu, Leko, and Utek. Bahu means happy, Leko means lazy, and Utek means brainy. They are my very best friends. Say hello to them or they will think you are very rude and eat you up.'

'Hello,' said Hanna weakly, by now almost convinced that the dogs would say 'hello' back.

Jik woke up with a start. He gave a gasp of shock when he saw the newcomer, and leapt defensively to Hanna's side. *'Nak apa?'* he demanded loudly in Indonesian. 'What do you want?'

Mini stared at him coolly, then switched her gaze to Hanna. 'Is he your guide? He's very rude!'

'Jik's our friend. My brother Ned is over here. He's sick—very sick. He needs help!'

Mini dropped to her haunches, and examined Ned closely. His eyes were still closed, his breathing shallow and irregular. It sounded as if it might stop at any moment. 'I will fetch my Uncle Irang,' she announced curtly. Then she stood up, turned, and disappeared into the jungle followed by her dogs.

14

Mini

'Who is that girl? Where did she come from?' Jik demanded as soon as he and Hanna were alone.

'Her name's Mini. I don't know where she came from. She just arrived. She shot that deer over there.'

Jik stared in disbelief at the motionless animal. 'With a gun?'

'With a knitting needle thing.'

For a moment he looked puzzled. Then the light dawned. 'You mean a poisoned arrow! You fire them from a blowpipe—see!'

He picked up Mini's spear, which she'd left resting against a rock, and showed it to Hanna. A neat hole had been drilled through its wooden shaft. 'Primitive people use them.'

'Mini's not primitive!' Hanna exclaimed, amazed that Jik even knew the meaning of the word. 'She speaks better English than you do!'

'Who says?' Jik exclaimed, hurt.

'I do—but your English is very good too!' she said hastily.

She dunked Ned's shirt into the stream and began to bathe him again. Apart from a slight intake of breath as the cold water came into contact with his hot skin, there was no indication that he knew who she was, or what she was doing. *'Hurry!'* she was praying, looking down at his flushed, expressionless face. *'Please hurry!'*

The wait seemed endless, but it can only have been twenty minutes at the most. A sudden strange hooting noise heralded Mini's return. With her was a wiry, light-skinned man wearing a pair of blue football shorts. He was bare-chested, and had an open, sympathetic face. He too was carrying a blowpipe, and had a *parang* slung from his waist.

He nodded at Hanna and Jik, and dropped to a crouch beside Ned. He felt his cheeks. *'Iah mayung keta,'* he said in low voice.

'My Uncle Irang says your brother is very ill. He has a fever caused by insects,' Mini said.

'Is it malaria?' Hanna asked anxiously.

'No, it is a different kind of fever. We have a special medicine to help this illness. It is made from the leaves of the *nyavung* tree. My uncle will bring your brother to our house and we will prepare this medicine for him.'

'We'll make a stretcher?' Jik asked, anxious to help.

Mini shook her head. 'There is no need. Uncle Irang will carry him. He is exceedingly strong.'

As if to illustrate her point, Irang bent, picked up Ned as if he weighed no more than a feather, and put him on his back. He said something to Mini who scuttled across the stream and stuffed the dead mouse-deer into a small rattan backpack she was wearing. Then she returned, grabbed her blowpipe, and followed by her three dogs, hurried to join her uncle.

Weak with hunger, Hanna and Jik found it hard to keep up with the pair as they sped off up the steep side of the valley. Fifteen minutes later they stumbled into a clearing. It was close to the ridge-line, with a panoramic view of the forest below.

In its centre was a hut. It had open sides, and was raised from the ground on spindly poles. Its roof was thatched with large forest leaves. It looked as if the merest puff of wind would blow it away.

As they approached it, Irang and Mini made the same strange hooting noise they'd made earlier back at the river. The noise was returned. It was obviously a form of greeting.

A woman emerged from the hut. She was wrapped in a sarong. Like Irang and Mini, she was fine-boned and light-skinned. 'This is my Auntie Tama,' Mini said. 'She will make the medicine for your brother.'

Auntie Tama greeted the children, glanced quickly at Ned, then grabbed a basket and a *parang*, and slipped away into the forest.

A notched pole led up to the house-platform. Still with Ned on his shoulders, Irang climbed nimbly up it, followed by Mini and, more cautiously, Jik and Hanna. Mini found a rattan mat, rolled it out, and Ned was lowered carefully onto it.

Hanna felt his forehead. His fever was getting worse again. She turned anxiously to Mini. 'How long will it take to make this medicine?'

'It will be very fast. I will make preparations.'

A clay hearth had been built at the front of the hut. On it a low fire was smouldering. Mini added extra wood and fanned it into flame. She found a small metal pot, poured some water from a bamboo storage tube into it, and put it on to boil. Then she sat back on her haunches to wait.

After a few minutes she pointed outside. 'See, Auntie Tama returns now!'

Her aunt emerged from the jungle and crossed to the hut at a quick jog. Her basket was full of small, sharp-pointed leaves. She took out a handful and swiftly pounded them to a pulp in a bamboo mortar and pestle. Then she added them to the boiling water. As it evaporated, a greeny-brown paste was left behind. This was mixed with more water and poured into a small plastic cup.

'The medicine is ready,' Mini announced. 'Now your brother must drink it.'

It was almost impossible to get Ned to open his mouth, let alone make him swallow anything, but eventually, by spooning it in a drop at a time, they managed to get some of it into him.

Would it work? A few years back Hanna would have been sceptical; but now, after their recent adventures, she was not so sure. So many of the world's most important medical drugs had been discovered deep inside tropical rainforests.

All she could do was hope that this was one of them.

Mini had no doubts. 'When he wakes up he will feel much revived,' she announced. 'Then we shall all live happily ever after.'

Where on earth had this tiny girl learned to speak such strange, old-fashioned English? At last Hanna had a chance to ask her.

'Po taught me,' Mini replied brightly. 'He told me that I must learn to speak correctly at all times. It is the mark of a young lady. Are you a young lady?'

'I'm . . . not sure,' Hanna replied, startled.

'Well, you should learn to become one! Po says it is most important.'

'Who is this Po?' Hanna asked, mystified.

'He is my *wali*—my guardian. Po is my special

name for him. He is very wise, and very kind. He is my best friend in the whole world! Would you like some *na'o* cakes? I expect you're very hungry.'

'I'm dam starving!' Jik admitted. He'd been silent up to now, anxious about Ned.

Hanna was hungry too—it was so long since they'd eaten! The word 'cake' conjured up a tantalizing vision of Mum's chocolate brownies, and Granny's Victoria sponge, oozing with cream and jam. Delicious!

Na'o cakes, on the other hand, looked anything but. They were made from smoked sago flour, mixed with pig's blood, then deep fried in pig fat, Mini explained as Auntie Tama prepared them.

Hanna's appetite vanished.

The cakes were served on individual leaves and looked like black oily hamburgers. They smelt rank. She forced herself to nibble at one of them.

To her amazement, it tasted quite nice—nutty, smoky, and surprisingly un-greasy. She even asked for a second helping. They'd roast the mouse-deer for supper, Mini told her, so there'd be plenty of food for later.

During the heat of the afternoon Irang and Tama went to sleep at the back of the hut, while the dogs snoozed in an untidy heap near the fire. Despite their exhaustion, Hanna and Jik didn't feel at all sleepy, and spent their time chatting with Mini.

She and Uncle Irang and Auntie Tama were Punan, she told them, the original people of the forest. Unlike the other tribes, they didn't grow rice, but hunted for game, and made sago starch from the trunks of special palm trees. The rest of their food—ferns, fruits, roots and leaves—they found in the jungle. It provided everything they wanted.

'Do you go to school?' Hanna asked, curious.

'Of course she doesn't go to dam school!' Jik exclaimed. 'She's far too young! How old are you, Mini?'

Mini looked affronted. 'I'm twelve.'

'Twelve? But you're so small!'

'That's why I'm called Mini. I have already explained that. And for your information, I *don't* go to school, but I *do* have lessons. Po teaches me. He's extremely clever and knows everything. We're doing quadratic equations this month. I love maths, don't you?'

For once, Jik was completely speechless.

Hanna asked about Mini's mother and father.

'They're dead,' she said. 'I am an orphan. My Uncle Irang and Auntie Tama cannot have babies, so Po sent me to live with them. I am now their child. Uncle Irang teaches me to hunt like a boy, and not to stay at home like a girl. This way, when he gets too old to hunt himself, I can get food for them. They are my favourite people in the whole world, except for Po, of course.'

Hanna was about to ask her more about the mysterious Po, when there was a sudden groan. Ned was waking up! She leapt to her feet and hurried to his side. His eyes flicked open. 'Where am I?' he asked in a slurred, confused voice.

'With friends.'

The answer seemed to satisfy him. 'I'm thirsty,' he complained.

Mini fetched some water, and the two girls eased him into a sitting position. They held the cup to his lips and he drank deeply. His body felt cooler now, the redness of his skin beginning to fade. Auntie Tama's medicine was obviously working. Hanna's spirits began to rise.

With Mini's help she gave him a second dose of medicine, and he went back to sleep. His breathing was deep and steady. 'Tomorrow he will be much better,' Mini announced confidently.

It was late afternoon before the adults woke up. Uncle Irang gutted and skinned the mouse-deer, and it was put to roast on racks over the fire. Auntie Tama boiled some sago and fried some fern tips to go with it.

They ate supper as the sun went down, and it

was delicious—except for the sago, which didn't just *look* like glue, but *tasted* like it too.

After they'd eaten, they sat around the fire and listened to the nightjars shrieking. What a difference twenty-four hours made, Hanna thought. Those same sounds, which had seemed so hostile as they'd cowered in the jungle the night before, had become almost comforting.

Now it was the children's turn to answer questions. Uncle Irang wanted to know where they had come from, and how they had come to be lost in the forest. Hanna wondered if it was wise to tell him everything. But the sight of their hosts' friendly, expectant faces in the flickering firelight, and the wonderful help they'd been given so far, convinced her that there was no danger.

It was a long story, and she began at the beginning, with Jik joining in from time to time. Mini translated for her uncle and aunt. As the story continued, Mini became increasingly excited. Eventually she could contain herself no longer. 'We have met your father and his friend!'

'You've met them?' Hanna was astonished.

'They came to our village. They wanted to buy sago flour and pig meat because their food was nearly finished. It was very thrilling! They were the first *laki mebung*—white people—I'd ever seen, apart from my Po of course, and now you!'

'Po's *white*?'

Mini nodded. 'He's from England. That's how I learned to speak correct English.'

'Jumping jellybeans, you've learned it dam well!' Jik exclaimed, with just a hint of jealousy in his voice. '*Almost* as good as me!'

Hanna ignored him. 'How were my father and Felix?' she asked Mini urgently. 'Were they well?'

'They were very hungry, but they were not sick. They spent a long time talking to Po.'

'What about?'

'I didn't hear. I was helping Ukun to prepare food for them.'

'Who's Ukun?'

'She's an old woman who looks after Po. Before they went away, Po gave them something. It was wrapped up in a cloth, so I couldn't see what it was. It must have been very important though. Po asked them to make sure it was placed in the right hands.'

'What did he mean by that?'

'I don't know. When your brother is strong enough, we can go to our village and ask Po himself. He will be exceedingly pleased to meet you.'

'Where did Hanna's father and Felix go after they'd finished talking to Po?' Jik asked.

Mini shrugged. 'Back to their camp on the Daha River, I guess.'

At the word *Daha*, Uncle Irang glanced up sharply. He said something quickly to Mini, who turned to the children. 'My uncle says the Daha River is a very dangerous place. Your father and his friend should not have come there.'

'Why not?' Hanna asked.

Mini hesitated. 'There are . . . stories. They say that anybody who takes gold from the Daha River is cursed and will probably die. When your father and his friend came to our village we told them about these stories, but they took no notice. They said it was just superstition.'

Hanna gave an involuntary shiver. If she'd been with Dad and Felix she'd have probably ignored the stories too. But now Felix was dead, and if they couldn't get Dad free, he soon would be as well . . .

'Do you believe these stories?' she asked Mini.

The little girl thought for a moment. 'I don't know,' she confessed. 'Perhaps it has something to do with the river's name. In the Punan language, *Daha* means blood. *The River of Blood.*'

15

An Extraordinary Story

They stayed in the little hut in the clearing for several more days. With the fresh meat that Uncle Irang brought in every morning, and with more doses of Auntie Tama's special medicine, Ned gradually began to get better.

Hanna found the wait very frustrating. The hut they were in was a *lamin,* a temporary shelter used on hunting expeditions. Mini's home village was two days' journey to the north; but with Ned still too weak to travel, it could have been a million miles away. She was desperate to meet Po and question him about the package he'd given to Dad and Felix. She became convinced that it held the key to Dad's freedom. What on earth was in it? And where was it right now? Only Po could provide the answers.

Exactly who was this mysterious Englishman?

One evening, while the children were sitting round the fire, Mini told them his story.

His real name was James Erskine, she said, and he'd first arrived in Borneo many years ago. He'd come because he was angry about the way the rainforest was being cut down by greedy logging companies on the Malaysian side of the border. He'd contacted the Punan tribes in the area and had fought alongside them to stop their hunting grounds being destroyed. The loggers had become furious, and had put a price on his head. Twice he'd been ambushed and nearly killed.

To save his life, he'd fled to East Borneo, crossing the border on foot. While he was walking through the forest one day, he'd come across an isolated hut. Inside, he'd found a young Punan woman about to give birth. Her husband had been killed by wild boar a few days previously, so she was all on her own. He'd stayed to help her. It was a very difficult birth, and the mother lost a lot of blood. She died soon afterwards.

'What about the baby?' Hanna asked.

'The baby was fine. She still is!'

A slow grin split Jik's face. 'Was the baby *you*, by any chance?'

Mini nodded triumphantly.

'Jumping jellybeans!'

Po had carried her through the jungle for two days and two nights, Mini went on. She'd needed milk but there was none. Eventually they'd arrived at a village. Luckily there was a woman living there who had recently given birth and had milk to spare. Though Mini was very weak, the woman had managed to feed her, and after a while she'd become strong enough to survive. When the people in the village heard about Po's bravery against the loggers they made him very welcome. They built a house for him, and asked him to stay. He became Mini's guardian. Po was her special name for him. It meant 'grandfather' in the Punan language, and was a mark of great respect.

'That's one of the most extraordinary stories I've ever heard,' Hanna said, when Mini had finally finished. 'Your Po must be a wonderful person.'

'Oh he is!' Mini exclaimed, her eyes sparkling. 'He's the most wonderful person in the whole wide world!'

Soon Ned was strong enough to join the other children for short walks in the forest. With Mini at their side, it was a different place—no longer strange and menacing, but full of fascinating sights and sounds. She pointed out three different types of squirrels—one of which could actually *fly* from branch to branch using flaps of skin on its legs—and told the children their Punan names: *pu'an, mega, telee.* They learned to distinguish between the noises made by different sorts of monkeys as they fed and quarrelled in the tree-tops; and learnt their Punan names too. Hanna kept a close lookout for her favourite animal—an orang-utan—but never saw one.

Mini taught them many other things too. How to move silently through the jungle, keeping your body supple and loose, weaving yourself between the branches, rather than crashing through them; how to mark your trail with *parang* slashes so you'd never get lost; and most fascinating of all, how to use the blowpipe.

Jik had been eyeing Mini's blowpipe enviously ever since she'd first shot the mouse-deer. And now Ned was feeling better, he too was keen to find out how it worked.

The little girl was more than willing to show them. 'It's called an *upit*,' she explained one afternoon when they were in the forest. 'It was made for me by a friend of Po, and it is very deadly.' She carefully extracted one of the knitting needle-like objects from her bamboo quiver. 'This is a *tahat*—a poison arrow. The sharp end has the poison on it, and the wide end fits inside the *upit*, see? But first I must bite it to make it tight.'

She chewed at the wide end of the arrow, then pushed it into the barrel of the blowpipe. It fitted firmly. 'What are you going to shoot?' Ned asked excitedly.

'You wait, see!'

A tree, hung with yellow fruit, was growing nearby. Mini crept up to it, peered into its branches for a minute or two. Then, holding the mouthpiece to her lips, took aim, and fired.

There was no sound except for a soft *pouft* as the arrow zipped out of the end of the barrel. Seconds later something fell to the ground. It was a large green lizard, impaled on the arrow like a kebab on a stick. 'This creature is very delicious,' Mini said, darting forward to pick it up. 'We will consume it later.'

The boys were almost speechless with astonishment and admiration.

They questioned her closely about the blow-pipe. It was made from a single piece of wood, she told them, and it took two or three days' hard work to drill a hole all the way through it. The poison came from the sap of a different tree, which was boiled until it was thick and black, and then smeared onto the end of the darts. It could kill even a large animal like a pig in a few minutes by stopping its heart from beating.

'How come it doesn't kill *us* when we eat the meat?' Hanna asked, puzzled.

'Because the hydrochloric acid in our tummies makes it safe,' Mini retorted. 'Isn't that obvious?'

She was not just a whizz at maths, but a whizz

at biology too, Hanna thought, looking at the tiny girl with new respect.

The children were desperate to try out the blowpipe for themselves—but Mini told them it was too dangerous to use her own poisoned arrows. Instead, Uncle Irang lent them a supply of new arrows that had not yet been dipped in poison to practise with.

They hung a small basket from the branch of a tree as a target, and Jik tried to hit it first. He put the blowpipe to his mouth, aimed carefully, inflated his cheeks like a balloon and made a very rude noise with his lips.

Instead of speeding to its target, the arrow slid gently out of the end of the blowpipe and plopped onto the grass at his feet.

Everybody burst into laughter—*except* Jik.

'You try!' he said crossly, thrusting the blowpipe at Ned, who was almost back to his old self again.

Ned tried. The result was the same.

Hanna was no better.

Laughing so hard that tears were trickling down her cheeks, Mini took back the blowpipe. 'You make your lips stiff,' she said, 'like you do when you're forced to kiss somebody you don't like. Then you say the word "Put!" as hard as you can. I'll show you.'

Her advice worked—eventually. By the end of

the afternoon the children were at least hitting the right tree, though none of them had yet managed to hit the basket. To become even half as good a shot as Mini—let alone Uncle Irang—would take huge amounts of time.

And time was something they didn't have.

Despite her joy at Ned's gradual return to health, and despite all the fun they were having with the blowpipe, Hanna was painfully aware that the days were slipping quickly past. Every morning, as she untied yet another knot in her piece of string, she renewed her vow to get Dad free. *'Please hurry up and get better!'* she silently urged her brother.

And he did.

16

Strangers in the Forest

On the morning that Ned was finally strong enough to travel, they woke before dawn, stowed the meagre contents of their little hut into home-made rattan backpacks, and set off east towards the rising sun, surrounded by excited dogs who somehow sensed they were going home. The forest was green and cool, echoing with the hoots of gibbons and the croak of hornbills. The path, which followed the ridge-line, was dry and level, and even Ned was able to make good time.

After an uneventful day's journey they stopped to make camp next to a clear, smooth-flowing stream. They cut saplings to build a sleeping plat-form, which they roofed with broad forest leaves. When they had finished, Uncle Irang took a small, circular net from his pack, and pausing to fill his pockets with pebbles, waded waist-deep into the river.

On the opposite bank was a fig tree laden with ripe fruit. Uncle Irang took a handful of pebbles and threw them into the water beneath the tree.

Instantly its glassy surface was broken by a flurry of fins. With an expert flick of his wrist, he flung out his net and hauled it in. Moments later three large fish were flapping on the bank. He repeated the process and two more joined them. They were fruit-eating fish, Mini explained to the children as they cleaned and de-scaled them ready for roasting over the fire. When the stones plopped into the water they thought they were figs falling from the tree and rushed towards them. They were simple to catch if you knew how!

They settled down to sleep early after a delicious supper of fish, followed by juicy figs. If all went well, Mini told them, they'd reach her village some time after noon the next day.

The following morning's trek was slow—Ned was tired after the previous day's journey. They rested for longer than usual after lunch. Soon after they got going again, Uncle Irang called an unexpected halt. He was staring at something at his feet. The children crowded round to see what it was.

An apparently random arrangement of twigs, leaves, and lengths of rattan, pinned together with a blowpipe arrow, had been set up next to the path. It looked like an outsized Christmas table decoration.

'What is it?' Ned asked Mini.

The little Punan girl, who'd been singing happily to herself as she walked along, looked suddenly serious. 'It's a *bata oroo*,' she replied. 'A message stick. It has been left here by some Punan people who have come this way before us. It tells us important things.'

'What important things?'

She spoke to her uncle. He looked worried. She translated his reply. 'The *bata oroo* tells us that there are strangers in the forest, and that we must be very careful. They have weapons. Guns.'

Hanna felt a prickle of fear. 'Who are these strangers?' she asked.

'The *bata oroo* does not say. But my uncle has seen a *pelakei kelit*—a bat eagle, and it is a very bad omen.'

Hanna stared around apprehensively. The jungle looked exactly the same as before. Nothing moved except a swarm of bees buzzing in and out of a hole in a nearby tree. Normally Uncle Irang would stop to harvest honey from any bees' nest they came across, using handfuls of smoking grass to put the insects to sleep. But today they would remain undisturbed.

He called the dogs to him with a soft hooting sound. 'Don't talk any more,' Mini whispered. 'It is too dangerous.'

The children nodded. The boys, clearly spooked,

moved up close. Hanna was conscious of her heart beating.

They abandoned the path and crossed the ridgeline. Beyond it was more jungle. The dogs fanned out ahead of them, slipping silently between the trees. They were being used as an early-warning system, Hanna realized. They would respond instantly to the smallest sniff of danger. Uncle Irang communicated with them constantly, using gentle hoots and whistles that to untrained ears sounded no different from the jungle noises around them. He took an arrow from his quiver and slipped it into his blowpipe. Hanna noticed that the one he'd selected had a sharp metal tip.

Midway through the afternoon they found a second message stick. This one had been constructed very recently—its stem was still damp with sap where the bark had been peeled back.

The news it gave was serious. Armed men had come to Mini's village. There had been fighting.

Uncle Irang broke into a run, the dogs staying just ahead of him. Auntie Tama and the children followed. 'I do hope my Po is safe!' Mini exclaimed as they sped along. 'I do hope he didn't try to fight these men! He's so stupid sometimes! So stupid and brave!'

'How much further?' Jik asked.

'Not far! Oh, I do hope he's safe!'

After a while Uncle Irang signalled to them to stop. He dropped to his stomach and squirmed silently through a patch of tall grass. He parted the stems and peered downwards. Looking over his shoulder, Hanna saw that they were at the edge of a shallow valley. Clustered beneath them were a dozen or so huts. They seemed to be deserted, apart from a few scrawny chickens scratching in the dirt.

After checking the scene several times, Uncle Irang lifted his hands to his mouth and made a deep, resonant hooting noise. He waited for a reply.

None came.

He hooted again, this time louder. One of the dogs whimpered anxiously, and was silenced with a hiss.

Eventually a faint answering hoot came from the jungle beyond the village. Uncle Irang said something to Auntie Tama in a low voice. 'The men with guns have gone,' Mini whispered to the children. 'But we must be still be very careful.'

A narrow path snaked down the valley side. They began a cautious descent. As they approached the huts, signs of a desperate struggle became clear. Clay hearths had been smashed; carefully-stacked bundles of firewood scattered.

Cooking pots and storage jars littered the ground, their contents spilled out. One hut had part of its roof missing.

Groups of villagers began to emerge from the forest and make their way slowly towards them. With the exception of a few elderly men, they consisted entirely of women and children. Several of the smaller children were shaking uncontrollably, clearly traumatized by what had happened. One woman, heavily pregnant, was clutching at her swollen stomach in distress. She looked as if she was going to give birth at any moment.

Hanna was puzzled. Where were all the younger men? She turned to ask Mini, but she was gone, running at high speed past the huts towards the head of the valley. 'I go to find my Po!' she yelled back over her shoulder.

Leaving Uncle Irang and Auntie Tama to deal with the returning villagers, Hanna, Ned, and Jik hurried after her.

The head of the valley was marked by a sheer cliff. A small waterfall tumbled over it. Taking what was obviously a familiar path, Mini skirted the cascade with its rainbow arc of spray, and scrambled upwards. The others followed. They found themselves on the edge of a large, clear pool overhung by giant forest trees. It was breathtakingly beautiful. Vivid, iridescent blue butterflies swirled and fluttered in the gentle breeze. Swallows—brown, not black like the ones at home—skimmed across the surface of the water. A swing hung from a nearby branch. It had been specially made for Mini, Hanna guessed.

Overlooking the pool was a hut, built—like the others in the village—from poles and leaves, though more sturdily constructed than most. Mini raced towards it yelling out Po's name.

She leapt up the notched entrance pole and into the hut. Hanna, Ned, and Jik climbed swiftly after her.

They stopped, aghast. Confronting them was a scene of total devastation. Chairs and tables had been overturned and smashed. Several large plastic boxes that had once contained books, folders, and camera equipment, had been emptied onto the floor. Exquisite drawings of jungle wildlife—gibbons, sun-bears, pythons—had been ripped from the walls and trampled underfoot. Whoever the attackers were, they had clearly been searching for something; and judging by the destruction they had caused, had failed to find it.

Mini was panicking now—half-screaming, half-sobbing: *'Po! Where are you? WHERE ARE YOU!'*

A groan. It was coming from the kitchen, a large, open shack built onto the back of the house.

The four children dashed into it. Lying on the floor next to the unlit hearth was an old woman, wearing a stained sarong. Her white hair was matted with blood. 'It's Ukun!' Minnie said frantically. 'She looks after Po.' She dropped to her knees beside the motionless body. 'Ukun, are you all right? What happened? Where's Po?'

At first Hanna thought the old woman was dead. But then her eyes slowly flickered open. 'He gone,' she just managed to say. 'Leopard Men take him.'

Leopard Men? What Leopard Men?

The children stared at Mini, waiting for an explanation. None came. Ukun was clearly in a bad way. Ned rushed to fetch water, and they gently bathed her head. The cut was deep, and she was almost certainly suffering from concussion. She should be in hospital, Hanna knew. But the nearest one was hundreds of miles away.

The cool water revived the old woman a little, and she was able to respond to Mini's frantic questioning. 'We hear much shouting, guns firing,' she said in broken English. 'I say to Po he must go to hide in the forest, but he does not listen. Then the Leopard Men come to this house. Po gets very angry. He goes up to them—never mind they have guns—and tells them to go away and leave us in peace. They push him to the ground, kick him with their boots. Then they come inside this house. They search for something, but they cannot find it. They take Po and drag him away. When I try to stop them they hit me on the head. After that I go *tayen*.'

'What's *tayen*?' Hanna asked.

'Unconscious,' Mini told her. 'Ukun, did they say where they were taking Po?'

'No. They say nothing . . . '

The old woman's voice had become faint. She was clearly unable to continue. Mini found a pot of brown ointment on a shelf and smeared some onto her wound. Then they wrapped her head in a clean cloth and half-led, half-carried her to her bedroom. 'Will she be all right?' Ned asked anxiously as they turned to leave her.

'I think so. Her daughter will take care of her. She is very skilful with medicine.' Mini glanced around apprehensively. 'Where's Jik?'

Her question was answered almost immediately. There was the sound of running footsteps and the Sea Gypsy boy burst into the room. He looked pale, like death. 'You better dam come with me!' he said.

Their hearts pounding, Mini, Hanna, and Ned followed him down the entrance pole. He led them behind the hut. There was a patch of open ground planted with aubergines, long beans, and squash.

Lying amongst the vegetables was what could have been a bundle of old clothes.

A cloud of buzzing flies betrayed the sickening truth.

It was a dead body.

The children stared at it aghast. 'Who is it?' Ned asked unsteadily.

Mini peered at the corpse's battered face. 'It's a man called Sanam,' she said, her voice betraying the relief she felt that it wasn't Po. 'He's from the village. He is Auntie Tama's cousin. He must have tried to fight the Leopard Men and they killed him.'

She was going to say more, but she didn't get the chance. There were footsteps. Voices. A crowd of villagers—Uncle Irang and Auntie Tama amongst them—came hurrying round the side of the hut.

They spotted the children first.

Then the body.

Their reaction was like nothing Hanna had ever heard, or ever wanted to hear again: a series of weird, agonized yelps, combining into a collective shriek of agony.

A stout woman, obviously Sanam's wife, rushed into the vegetable patch and took the dead man into her arms. She was joined by half a dozen hysterical small children.

Mini dashed past them, heading for Uncle Irang. She was shouting at him in a mixture of Punan and English. '*Mah Po irai ke? Where's Po? What have they done with Po?*'

He spoke to her briefly, not taking his eyes from the terrible scene before him. 'What did he say?' Ned asked anxiously, when she returned.

'They took Po away,' she said, in between sobs. 'They also took Petrus and Liang, who are the strongest men in the village. They put iron shackles on their legs and joined them up with chains. Then they forced them to walk into the forest.'

'Where to? Where were they being taken to?'

Before Mini could reply, a new sound joined the screams and sobs of the villagers: a mechanical drone, getting louder by the second. A small plane, painted a dull jungle green, passed low overhead. It was obviously heavily laden, struggling to gain height.

Its shape was sickeningly familiar.

It was the plane they'd tried to hijack back at the jungle airstrip. Hanna knew where it was heading: the mysterious 'Arena' where Felix had met his brutal end.

17

The Leopard Men

'Tell us about these Leopard Men,' Hanna said urgently to Mini. 'Who exactly are they?'

Darkness had fallen. The children were sitting on the platform at Uncle Irang's hut, watching the procession of flaming torches that accompanied Sanam's body as it was carried into the centre of the village by weeping relatives.

'Nobody knows,' Mini said quietly. 'They come from the forest, usually about the time of the rice harvest, and take people away.'

'Are they blood collectors?' Ned asked. 'Are they *bali saleng*?'

Mini shook her head violently. '*Bali saleng* don't exist. They're just a myth—Po told me that. Only stupid villagers believe in them. But the Leopard Men are real. They wear army uniforms, and have powerful guns. Sometimes a hunter spots them and warns people so they can hide. But often there is no warning. Always they take only men. Never women.'

'And nobody ever comes back?'

Tears glistened on Mini's cheeks. 'Never. Some people say that they are taken to be slaves—forced to work until they die—but nobody knows for certain. Once upon a time, many years would pass between each raid. But now the Leopard Men come to the villages more and more often. Anybody who tries to resist them is killed. Soon there will be no more Punan people left. Oh why didn't Po go and hide in the forest when he had the chance? Why didn't he do what Ukun told him?'

'Has nobody ever tried to stop this?' Hanna asked, appalled.

'Po has tried, many times. Once he went downriver all the way to Sangabera to tell the Government, but they wouldn't listen to him. They said he was breaking the law by staying with the Punan, and tried to send him back to England. He had to pay a lot of money to escape and return to us. Nobody can stop this thing! Nobody!'

Mini's tiny body was racked by fresh sobs. Hanna took her into her arms to comfort her. Her mind was spinning. Something very big was clearly happening up here—something very sinister. The army was presumably involved. And so— judging by Dodi—were the police. Felix had been a victim. Now Po was captured too. And if it hadn't been for the fire ants—plus a large slice of luck—she, Ned, and Jik would have certainly joined them.

But *why?*

If it wasn't to collect their blood, what were all these people being kidnapped *for?* There had to be a very good reason.

Somehow they had to find the mystery package that Po had given to Dad and Felix. Hanna was convinced that it held the key to everything.

Mini's sobs had faded now, replaced by the occasional sniff. Hanna turned to face her. 'We need your help,' she said, explaining her feelings about the package. 'I'm certain it's still at Dad's camp on Blood River, hidden away somewhere. Can you take us there?'

'Will it help to get Po back?'

'I'm sure it will. Everything is linked up, though I don't know exactly how. The package must be important or Po wouldn't have given it to Dad and Felix and asked them to take it with them. If we can find it, I believe we can somehow stop this thing happening and save everybody's lives.'

Mini was quiet for a moment. Then she nodded quickly. 'I will come with you. I will do *anything* to save my Po. When should we start?'

'Tomorrow. As soon as the sun rises.'

The mourning ceremony for Sanam had begun. A circle of fires was lit, bathing the village in

146

flickering yellow light. From the hut of the dead man a strange, haunting song rose up. One by one the inhabitants of the other huts joined in, accompanied by the wail of nose-flutes. It was a death song, Mini said. It was telling the dead man not to be afraid on his long journey into the spirit world.

The body, wrapped in intricately woven mats, was brought down and placed inside the circle of fire. Weeping villagers surrounded it, rocking backwards and forwards on their haunches.

As the children watched, an old man entered the circle. He had pierced ears, hung with heavy brass rings. He was clutching a stick decorated with tassels of peeled bark. He was a *dayong,* Mini said—a magic man.

The *dayong* began a slow, shuffling dance. He was talking to the dead man as he danced, his voice occasionally rising to a shout. 'We Sea Gypsies have a magic man like this on our islands,' Jik said admiringly. 'He is an exceedingly dam powerful person.' There was a note of homesickness in his voice.

The chanting and dancing would go on till dawn, Mini told them. After that the body would be carried into the jungle, where it would be left to join the spirits.

'Won't it be buried?' Ned asked, puzzled.

She shook her head. 'No.'

'But won't things *eat* it? Animals? Insects?'

'Yes.' She turned away. The topic was obviously closed.

Despite the noise of the chanting, the children managed to grab a few hours of sleep before Uncle Irang and Auntie Tama, who'd joined the mourners, eventually returned. They looked sad and exhausted in the early morning light. Uncle Irang was horrified when Mini told him about their plan to go to Blood River. It was too dangerous, he protested. But Mini persisted, and eventually, reluctantly, he agreed. She would stop at nothing to get Po back, he knew. He would come with them, he said, but he was needed for the move.

'What move?' Ned asked.

The village was being abandoned, Mini explained. A new one would be built on the other side of the mountain. After what had happened there were too many bad spirits in this place for people to stay.

Auntie Tama packed food for them—sago flour and sticks of smoked deer meat. Mini collected extra supplies of arrows for her blowpipe. Hanna and the boys were given *parangs* to sling from their waists. In their rattan backpacks were fishing nets, sleeping mats, and several juicy pomelos from a tree growing behind the hut. Before they left, Uncle Irang embraced each of them in turn. They were to be brave, he said. Brave and strong. Only if they were brave, would they find success.

As the sun rose above the rim of the forest, the four children climbed down the notched entrance pole to the ground, waved goodbye to the two grown-ups, and accompanied by Mini's three excited dogs, set off towards Blood River.

As they skirted the village, they passed a slow procession of mourners. Sanam's body was being carried to its final resting-place deep in the jungle.

18

The Golden Man

The journey to Blood River took three days. The landscape became increasingly mountainous, the path twisting steeply upwards between jagged limestone rocks. As they climbed higher the temperature dropped, and at night the children and the dogs were forced to huddle together for warmth.

Though they remained fiercely loyal to Mini, the three dogs adopted Hanna, Ned, and Jik as their own, and were always ready for a pat or a game. They really did live up to their names. Bahu seemed to be permanently happy, her tail wagging merrily all day long. Leko was lazy, always the last to wake up in the mornings.

But of all the dogs, Hanna liked brainy Utek the best. He was brown like the other two, but had one black ear, which hung down over his left eye, making him look a bit like an old-fashioned pirate. He invariably took the lead as they went along, freezing in his tracks if he spotted any potential danger, and pointing at it with his outstretched nose. He had only one thing wrong with him: he snored loudly at night, and insisted on sleeping right next to Hanna!

They made good progress. Ned had finally got all his old strength back, and was moving as swiftly and easily as the others. They made camp early each afternoon, leaving plenty of time to build a sleeping platform, and to try to catch something for supper before darkness fell. The first night Jik took a net into a nearby marshy area and returned with a dozen large bullfrogs. They tasted a bit like roast chicken, and were delicious. Next day Mini shot a blue-eyed pigeon with her blow-pipe. There wasn't much meat on it, but it was still better than week-old smoked deer.

That night, after supper, they talked about Blood River. Mini had been there once, she told them, on a hunting expedition with Uncle Irang.

'Is the water red?' Jik asked.

She laughed. 'No, it's a normal colour.'

'So why's it called Blood River then?'

'I told you, there are stories. Legends.'

'Go on, tell us one!'

'Yes, tell us!' Ned urged, joining in with his friend.

The little Punan girl looked uncomfortable. 'I only know one of them. Uncle Irang knows a lot more.'

151

'So tell us the one you *do* know,' Ned said exasperatedly.

Mini took a deep breath. 'OK, but it's not very nice! It is the story of *Laki Mat*—the Golden Man. It happened many years ago. One day a stranger arrived in the lands of the Punan. His body was made only of gold and blood. Among the Punan at that time there was a warrior called Raja Mutang. He was brave, but he was also stupid. He thought the gold would make the Punan very rich, and they could buy many things from the Chinese traders. So one night he took his sword and went to where the Golden Man was sleeping and killed him. What Raja Mutang didn't know was that the Golden Man was really a *pehnako,* an evil spirit. As the Golden Man's head rolled from his body, it began to rain. But the rain was not water—it was blood.'

'That's gross!' Ned exclaimed.

'I told you it's not a nice story. The rain turned into a great storm of blood, and soon the whole village was washed away. All the people were drowned, including Raja Mutang. Nothing was left except a small river. After a while, the blood disappeared and the river ran clear. In its bed was all the gold from the body of the Golden Man. Over the years many people have tried to get this gold. Most of them have died.'

Hanna shivered. She peered out into the darkness. Strange green lights winked and glowed on the forest floor. They were luminous mushrooms, she knew, but they looked like demonic, evil eyes staring back at her.

The Golden Man might be just a legend.

But in the jungle, at night, legends were very easy to believe.

They reached Blood River at noon the following day. The gold workings looked nothing like Hanna had imagined. Somehow she'd pictured Dad and Felix up to their waists in water, swilling sand around in frying pans, like old-time prospectors.

But this was more like an industrial site. Moored in midstream, on a makeshift raft, was an ancient-looking engine. Pipes led down from it into the murky water. Beyond it was a steep wooden chute—like an outsize playground slide.

Mini explained to the others what everything was—she'd visited gold workings with Po in the past. The engine was called a compressor. It acted like a large vacuum cleaner, sucking up silt and mud and gold from the river bed and squirting it into the wooden chute. The chute was lined with a carpet. The gold particles were much heavier than the mud, and sank to the bottom where they got trapped in the bristles of the carpet. The gold was then washed out with clean water and collected in a tray.

'Cool!' said Ned.

Except it wasn't. Blood River didn't seem like an exciting place at all—and certainly not an evil one. It was just scruffy and depressing. Empty oil-drums and plastic sacks littered its banks. A flat-bottomed boat, presumably used by Felix and Dad to ferry the machinery upstream, lay sunken and abandoned at the water's edge. Creepers and elephant grass were already invading the site.

Hanna stared around her apprehensively. This really was their last chance. If they drew a blank here the consequences didn't bear thinking about. But how on earth were they going to find *anything* in this godforsaken place?

There was a shout from Jik. He was pointing at something on the valley side. Almost hidden by thick undergrowth was a hut. An overgrown path led up to it. It had to be the place that Dad and Felix had been living in!

The two boys raced towards it, followed closely by Hanna, Mini, and the dogs.

It was solidly built, with a wide veranda over-looking the river. Hanna could imagine Dad and Felix sitting there when work was done for the day, watching the sun set over the jungle, no doubt talking about home. What had happened to them was so unfair!

Ned pushed at the door. It creaked open. Hanna peered inside. She'd been expecting devastation—overturned furniture, scattered papers, smashed cooking pots—all the signs of a violent raid.

But the place was untouched. There were books on the shelves, pictures on the walls, a *parang* hanging in its sheath from a nail on a post. There was even a half-drunk bottle of beer on the table. It was as if Felix—or Dad—had just stepped outside, and would be back at any moment. Hanna felt the hairs on her neck prickle. It was quite spooky.

The boys didn't seem to share her concern. They marched boldly inside, pulling open the shutters, flooding the room with light. There was a small kitchen at the rear; and two bedrooms. It was obvious which one had been Dad's—lined up on a ledge next to his mattress were framed pictures of Mum, Ned, Jik, and herself back at the cottage in England. The sight of their happy, smiling faces brought tears to her eyes. Would they ever all be together again?

'See what I have discovered!'

It was Mini's voice, coming from Felix's room. The children hurried to join her. In one corner, its door hanging open, was a small safe.

It was empty.

Hanna's heart sank. It was clear now what must have happened. The Leopard Men had surprised Felix while he was outside—probably down at the river. Before marching him away to the airstrip, they'd taken him up to the hut at gunpoint and forced him to open the safe. There would have been very little gold inside it—Dad had got that. But there would have been other valuable things— passports, permits, return air tickets.

And Po's package.

Unless Dad had taken it downriver with him—in which case the police would have seized it when they'd arrested him—it would surely have been locked in here. Hanna stared at the others in anguish. She'd pinned so much hope—*too* much hope—on finding the package. Now they'd never know what was inside it.

It was gone for good.

If Ned shared her despair, he didn't show it. 'Don't worry,' he said brightly. 'I bet there are loads of other clues in this place. Things that are just as important as that stupid package. Why don't we each take a room and search it thor- oughly. We're bound to come up with something.'

Jik nodded. 'I bet I find a big clue first. My eyes are like X-ray vision machines!'

His remark made everybody giggle. Feeling a

156

little better, they decided that Jik would take the kitchen, Mini and Ned would take a bedroom each, and Hanna would search the living room. If anybody found anything they were to shout out. 'Remember, use your brains as well as your eyes,' Hanna told them.

'Yes, boss,' said Ned, standing to attention and saluting.

That made them all smile again.

Their smiles didn't last.

Though they searched all afternoon they didn't find a single clue. To Hanna's disappointment the books on the shelves were mostly about mining. She had been hoping to find a diary or a journal amongst them, but the only handwritten things she came across were notes saying such stuff as 'Wash out the tailings, Wednesday p.m.' Apart from a small mountain of dirty clothes, and a broken two-way radio, there wasn't much else. Eventually it became too dark to see and they had to stop. Exhausted and discouraged, the children gathered on the veranda. If there were any clues to be found at Blood River, they certainly weren't inside the hut.

'We can't just give up,' Ned said. 'There must be somewhere else to look.'

'Like where?' Jik asked.

Night fell. They managed to get a fire going in the hearth and boiled some rice they'd found in the kitchen. Jik discovered a tin of sardines with his X-ray eyes, and they added those to the rice. Usually food cheered everybody up, but that night it didn't. They went to bed early, dragging the mattresses onto the veranda, where it was cooler. They rigged up a mosquito net to keep out the worst of the insects, and lay down next to each other. They felt too depressed to talk, and one by one, drifted off into a troubled sleep.

19

Brainwave

Hanna woke with a start. A cold, damp nose was pressed against her cheek through a hole in the mosquito net. It was Utek. He looked at her expectantly for a moment or two, then quickly scampered to the edge of the veranda and peered downwards. Puzzled, she untangled herself from the net and went to see what he was staring at.

It was early dawn, the valley bottom swathed in a pale mist. The abandoned gold workings, so scruffy in the clear light of day, loomed through the whiteness like the ruins of some strange lost civilization. Utek, his nose outstretched, was pointing away to the left. Hanna peered intently in the direction he indicated. 'What is it?' she asked him softly. 'What can you see?'

The dog continued to point, the hairs on his back bristling. There was definitely something down there—but what was it?

Suddenly the mist thinned. Crouched at the river's edge was a bent, black figure. It was staring into the river. For one heart-stopping moment Hanna thought it was human.

But then it moved.

It was a bear.

A large, black bear.

She quickly woke the others. They crowded to the edge of the veranda to take a look. It was a *buang*—a sun bear, Mini told them. It was the most dangerous animal in the whole of Borneo, and would attack without warning.

'What should we do?' Ned asked her anxiously.

'Stay quiet. It will go away.'

The children stayed quiet—very quiet. Unfortunately Utek didn't. Unable to control his excitement, he gave a strangled yelp.

The bear glanced up, spotted them, opened its mouth and let out a loud, angry roar. Its sharp white teeth glistened in the early morning light. Then, balancing on its hind legs, it quickly waded across the river, and strode up the path towards them.

'It's coming here!' Ned gasped. 'It's coming to the hut!'

Mini didn't seem concerned. She spoke calmly to the dogs. Needing no second bidding, they leapt off the veranda and raced down the path to confront the animal. For a short while they stayed out of its reach, barking at it furiously. Then they separated, and began to dart in at it from different directions, snapping at its heels. It seemed as if they must get caught by its razor-sharp claws, but they were always too quick for it. After a few minutes the bear gave up the contest, and snarling furiously, lumbered off into the forest.

The dogs wanted to follow, but Mini called them off. Wagging their tails triumphantly, they raced back up to the veranda. 'We must give them a big clap,' she announced, patting them proudly.

To the relieved children, giving the dogs a round of applause seemed the least they could do.

'It's the first dam time I've ever seen a sun bear,' Jik confessed, when the excitement had died down a little.

'Me too,' said Ned. 'And I don't want to see one again in a hurry!' He broke off suddenly, and glanced keenly at his friend. 'Repeat what you just said, Jik,' he ordered.

'Repeat what?'

'About the bear.'

Jik looked puzzled. 'I said, it's the first dam time I ever saw a sun bear.'

Ned twisted towards his sister. 'What does that sound like?'

Hanna was as puzzled as Jik. 'What does *what* sound like? Please stop being so mysterious!'

'You remember you said that Dad was trying

to tell you something back in that courtroom in Sangabera, but you couldn't hear what it was?'

Hanna nodded, still wondering what he was getting at. 'I thought he was asking for *some beer*, but he couldn't possibly have been.'

'What if he was actually saying *sun bear*? It sounds almost the same as *some beer*. And what if he was referring to this same sun bear that just tried to attack us?'

'I still don't understand,' Hanna said.

Ned gave an exasperated sigh. 'If you had something very important to hide, where's the safest place you could possibly put it? Inside a *bear's den*, of course!'

'Sun bears don't have dens,' Mini pointed out. 'They live in trees.'

'OK, in a bear's *tree*. All we've got to do is find where this creature lives, and I'll bet Po's package is there too!'

Hanna's heart began to beat wildly. The fact that the two sets of words sounded almost the same might just be a coincidence, but it was unlikely. She stared at her brother in wonder. Had Ned just had one of his famous brainwaves? 'It'll be very dangerous,' she said.

'Of course it'll be dangerous! That's the whole point. Dad was counting on us to be brave enough not to let a little danger bother us.'

'But we don't know where this bear lives,' Jik pointed out. 'There's a lot of dam jungle out there.'

Mini grinned. 'No problem! We'll ask the dogs. They'll take us there straight away!'

There was no time to lose. Pausing only to swallow a few mouthfuls of left-over rice for breakfast, the children pulled on their trainers and grabbed their *parangs*. Mini reached for her blowpipe, and they followed the excited dogs out of the hut.

Utek picked up the bear's scent straight away, dashing into the undergrowth in the direction it had just disappeared. They had to call him back sharply. He might be brainy, but he didn't seem to realize they wanted him to show them where the bear had come from, *not* where was it going to!

They quickly traced its tracks back down to the river, and waded across. The dogs found the scent again without difficulty on the other side and set off up the valley. The bear had been following a well-worn path, every now and then making diversions into the jungle, presumably in search of food. Once, it had broken into a termite mound to help itself to the insects inside.

How far would they need to travel before they reached its nest, Hanna wondered anxiously. Sun bears were nocturnal, so it could easily have been wandering about all night. If so, wouldn't its scent get fainter as time went on, and perhaps fade away completely before they found it?

The dogs seemed to have no worries on that score. Their noses to the ground, they raced confidently onwards.

About a kilometre above the gold workings, a small tributary stream joined the main river. The dogs turned up a narrow path running alongside it.

The children followed cautiously. The rocks were slippery, and the thought of meeting an angry bear was far from pleasant. Suddenly Utek stopped. His body had gone rigid. He was pointing at something with his nose. They scrambled up to join him.

They would never have spotted the cave without the dog's help. Its entrance was a narrow gash in the hillside, almost completely hidden by trailing vegetation. There were paw-marks in the soft mud leading into it. Despite what Mini had said about sun bears nesting in trees, there was no doubt that this was where their particular bear lived.

But was it at home?

Hanna scarcely had time to form the question in her mind, before the dogs decided to answer it. They scampered into the cave and disappeared.

'Get ready!' Mini hissed. 'If it is at home, I think

it will come out very soon!' She pulled an arrow from her quiver, chewed its end and pushed it into her blowpipe.

Feeling a bit like medieval knights, Hanna, Ned, and Jik drew their *parangs* and waited, hearts pounding. 'Please don't let it be in there!' Hanna heard herself saying, wondering what she would do if the bear attacked.

Their wait was a short one. Minutes later, tongues flapping, tails wagging, the three dogs raced out into the sunshine.

Ned let out a whoop of joy. 'It's safe. We can go inside!'

'Not yet!' Mini disappeared into the trees clutching her *parang*. There was the sound of chopping. She returned soon afterwards with a freshly-split log. She swiftly scraped out its resinous centre, which she twisted round the ends of four stout sticks. Then she took a cigarette lighter from the waterproof pouch on her belt, and lit them. They burned brightly. She handed one to each of the children. 'Now we can see,' she announced.

Jik was speechless with admiration.

It was the smell the children noticed first as they entered the cave. The musty odour of bear was unmistakable. But mixed with it was another, much worse stink. It was only when they got further inside that they realized what it was.

Lit by the glow from their torches were countless thousands of bats. Most of them were hanging upside down from the roof; but many more, disturbed by the light, were swooping and fluttering in the confined space, filling the air with their high-pitched squeaks.

The smell came from their droppings.

A thick, stinking carpet of bat poo coated the floor and every available flat surface.

If it had just been poo, it would have been bearable. But it wasn't. It was seething with insects—beetles, cockroaches, centipedes—and fat, white, wriggling maggots.

As Hanna's feet sank into the revolting mess, the insects began to scuttle over the tops of her trainers and up her bare legs. It felt as if she was being eaten alive.

Fighting a desire to scream, she urged Mini and the boys onwards. Dad and Felix surely wouldn't have left anything important in the middle of this lot!

Mercifully, the bats got fewer as they ventured further into the cave. Daylight was no longer visible now. Thank goodness for Mini's home made torches—without them, the darkness would have been total.

After a while the walls of the cave began to close in, until it became little more than a narrow passage. The bear smell was much stronger now, masking the stink of the bats. The dogs raced ahead excitedly. Squeezing through a final gap, the children found themselves in a circular chamber. Beyond it was solid rock. They could go no further.

They didn't need to.

Even to their untrained eyes, it was obvious that this was where the bear lived. The floor was lined with dried grass and fur, making a comfortable bed. Piles of gnawed bones lay to one side. They could well imagine its owner sleeping peacefully here during daylight hours until it was time for the night's hunting and scavenging. And maybe—if it was a female—even giving birth to cubs.

If Ned's theory was correct, this was surely where Po's package was hidden.

Conscious that the bear could return at any time, the children began a frantic search. They drew a blank. There were few places where anything might be hidden, and there was nothing apart from bedding and bones on the floor.

They were close to giving up when a loud exclamation from Jik made them glance up sharply. He was pointing at the roof.

Suspended from a twisted stalactite was a rattan basket. Just visible inside it was something wrapped in a stained cloth.

It *had* to be Po's package! Felix must have hung it up there out of the bear's reach.

There was just one problem: how could they possibly get it down?

Mini came up with the best idea. They must climb onto each other's shoulders like circus performers, she said.

Hanna volunteered to be at the bottom. Jik would climb onto her shoulders, then Mini, who was the smallest and lightest, would climb onto his. Ned would help them to get into position, and try to catch anybody if they fell.

It was easier said than done, but eventually they managed it.

Mini stretched up towards the basket. She was still too short. 'My blowpipe!' she ordered.

Ned handed it up to her. She hooked its tip under the basket's rim and pushed.

It swung for a moment, then tumbled downwards.

So did Mini.

Reacting with extraordinary speed, Ned flung himself across the cave and caught her as she fell. He held on to her for a split second, then lost his balance, collapsing backwards. The two of them rolled across the floor before finally coming to a stop against one of the walls.

It didn't matter. Apart from a few minor

bruises, neither of them was hurt. They burst into relieved laughter.

Picking bits of fur and bedding out of their hair, they scrambled to their feet. Jik jumped down from Hanna's shoulders.

They reached for the basket with trembling hands. Now, at last, they would learn the secret of Po's mystery package!

They were about to unwrap it, when a sudden yelp from Utek made them glance up sharply. The three dogs were standing at the entrance to the chamber, their fur bristling. They had heard—or smelt—something.

Moments later, the children found out what it was. A low growl rumbled out of the darkness.

The bear was coming back!

20

A Desperate Struggle

'What do we do now?' Jik exclaimed, wide-eyed.

'I don't know!' Hanna yelled back.

They unsheathed their *parangs*, but they were useless. They'd be ripped to pieces by the bear's claws before they could get close enough to do anything. And even if they managed to land a blow, they'd just wound it, which would make it more dangerous.

At least Mini had her blowpipe. A well-aimed arrow would surely stop the creature in its tracks.

They turned towards her expectantly, but she let out an anguished cry. 'My *upit* is broken!' She held up its shattered remains. It had been smashed when she and Ned had crashed to the floor.

Now they really *were* in trouble!

There was a second growl—louder than the first, and much angrier. The dogs were going crazy now, yelping and barking. Would the bear remember what had happened to it earlier that morning, and back off?

It didn't.

As its black bulk filled the entrance to the chamber, its growls turned into snarls of fury. It had spotted the children.

Jik grabbed a flaming torch and thrust it at its face.

It hesitated. Backed off.

That was when the dogs attacked.

Bahu and Leko dived for its hind legs. It kicked them away angrily.

Then it was Utek's turn.

With a prodigious leap he launched himself at the animal's throat.

The bear roared with fresh fury, and tried to bat him away. But Utek clung on tenaciously.

Desperate to get rid of its attacker, the bear lurched forwards, crushing the brave dog against the cave wall. Its teeth closed on his hindquarters.

He let out a howl of agony and tried to escape, but he couldn't.

'Utek!' Mini screamed hysterically. 'Utek!'

What happened next seemed to take place in slow motion. The little Punan girl sprinted to the bear and flung herself onto its back.

It tried to shake her off, but somehow she clung on, riding it like a bucking horse.

There was something in her hand.

It was a blowpipe arrow.

Gripping it like a dagger, she stabbed it into the bear's flank.

Bellowing with pain and fury, the animal rose onto its hind legs, trying to get at her, but still she refused to be shaken off. It was pirouetting in its frenzy.

Suddenly, it stopped turning.

It shook its head twice, as if to clear it.

Then, with a puzzled look on its face, it pitched forwards, and was still.

Hanna sprinted across to Mini and pulled her clear. The little girl was shaking with shock. Hanna didn't know whether to praise her or scold her.

'Is it dead?' Ned asked fearfully.

Mini shook her head. 'I don't think so. The poison is not strong enough. It is sleeping.'

'That means it'll wake up?'

'Some time.'

Ned tried to ask her exactly when, but Mini was no longer paying attention. She was staring wildly round the cave. 'Where's Utek?' she asked in an anguished voice. Bahu and Leko were standing guard over the unconscious bear, but her favourite dog was nowhere to be seen.

It was Jik who eventually spotted him. He was trapped under the fallen animal. Terrified that it might wake up suddenly, the two boys quickly rolled the bear off him.

172

A glance at the dog's twisted, bloody body told them that he had only minutes to live. His spine had been bitten through; his hind legs almost severed. Mini dropped to her knees beside him, tears streaming down her face. She was talking softly to him in the Punan language.

She reached out to stroke him.

As Utek felt the pressure of her fingers, he raised his head and gently licked her hand.

Then his friendly brown eyes closed for the last time.

It took a while for Mini to accept that he was dead. When she did, her grief came out as anger. 'I hate this bear!' she screamed. 'I hate it! I'm going to kill it!'

She grabbed a *parang* from her belt, but Jik wrestled it away from her. He was pointing at the unconscious animal. 'Look!' he said.

The bear's right paw was withered and useless. Some time in the past it had been caught in a vicious wire snare that had cut deep into its limb, stopping the blood flow. The wire was still in place, the flesh around it raw and bloody where the animal had tried to chew it free.

So that was the reason it had chosen a cave for its home! It had no alternative. It was unable to climb trees to make a nest, or hunt properly. No wonder it was so aggressive. It must be in permanent agony.

Despite what it had done to Utek, Mini's anger left her as soon as she realized how badly injured the creature was. 'We must get that thing off it quickly,' she said urgently. 'It will wake up soon!'

Fighting the urge to flee, Hanna hurried to help her.

It took them a long time to release the snare—the wire was thick, and tightly twisted; but eventually they succeeded. The bear would never regain the use of its paw, but at least it would no longer be in pain.

Now it really was time to go!

Mini went to where Utek was lying and took his battered body into her arms. Ned grabbed the precious basket and slung it over his shoulder. Hanna and Jik picked up the flickering torches. They were edging past the bear when their worst fears began to come true. Its eyes jerked open, and it gave an angry snort.

'Let's get out of here!' yelled Ned.

The four friends raced out through a cloud of screeching bats towards daylight and safety.

21
Po's Package

They 'buried' Utek in the jungle, wrapping him in leaves and placing him on a low platform of branches that Mini swiftly constructed. It was close to a marshy area alive with the croaking of frogs. 'He will be happy here,' the little girl announced, fresh tears wetting her cheeks. 'When he was a puppy his favourite game was chasing frogs. Now he will be able to chase them for ever.'

They stood in silence with their eyes closed, for a minute or two. Then Mini turned and spoke to Bahu and Leko in the Punan language. The two dogs responded with a series of tiny yaps and whines. 'What did you say to them?' Hanna asked, intrigued.

'I told them that now Utek has gone, they must take his place. Bahu must become less happy and more fierce. And Leko must be less lazy and do more work. They agreed.'

'You can understand what they say?' Ned asked, astonished.

Mini nodded. 'Of course. All you have to do is listen.'

Despite her sadness at Utek's death, Hanna began to tingle with excitement as they made their way back to the hut. It was time for Po's package to yield up its secrets!

The basket was difficult to open—its top had been sewn tightly shut with rattan strips. Eventually they had to use a knife to cut through it. Inside was a plastic bag, and inside that, was a flat rectangular box, wrapped in a cloth.

'That's Ukun's old sarong!' Mini exclaimed when she saw the cloth. 'I'd recognize it anywhere. This is certainly the parcel Po gave to your father and his friend!'

With trembling fingers, Hanna unwrapped the cloth, to reveal a red box-file. It was twisted out of shape, its binding split. The damage must have happened when it had crashed onto the cave floor. But to everyone's relief, its contents seemed to be unharmed.

Hanna took them out and spread them carefully on the veranda floor.

On top was a brown envelope marked: *To Whom It May Concern.*

Next was a journal bound in battered leather labelled: *Observations.*

Finally, there was a large-scale map of central Borneo.

They decided to read the letter first. Hanna opened it carefully. It consisted of two sheets of paper covered in neat handwriting, which an excited Mini said was definitely Po's. It was dated six weeks earlier, and, like the envelope, was headed: 'To Whom It May Concern'.

Hanna read it out loud to the others.

'My name is James Erskine. For the last twelve years I have lived with the Punan people in their tribal lands to the north of the Barang River. They are gentle and peaceful people, spending their time hunting for game and gathering plants from the rainforest for food and medicine.

'In recent years they have become the victims of a series of unprovoked attacks by an armed gang calling themselves Laki Kuli—Leopard Men. These men, most of whom wear army uniforms, can be identified by an overgrown, claw-like fingernail on their left hands.

'The attacks are brutal, and happen without warning. Their object appears to be kidnapping. The captives are usually taken in chains to a jungle airstrip, and flown out by light aircraft to an unknown destination.

'For the past three years I have kept a journal, in which I have recorded the timing and locations of these attacks, and the names of the victims involved. Attacks

177

appear to be concentrated at the time of the rice har-
vest.

'*In January this year, there was a big gathering of
Punan in a valley close to the Babak River. The Leopard
Men attacked this gathering and twenty men were kidnapped. Because of the large number of prisoners,
they were not airlifted out on this occasion, but taken
into the jungle on foot.*

'*I tracked them, undetected, for several days. They
were heading north-east towards the Darma Range, a
remote and little-explored upland area in central
Borneo. Their destination was a mysterious double-
peaked mountain called Batu Kuli—Leopard Rock. At
its foot is a heavily-guarded complex of buildings
referred to by the Leopard Men as the "Arena". In conversations I overheard, they spoke of this place with
considerable awe, which suggests that it may be of reli-
gious or ritual significance to them.*

'*Because of heavy security I was unable to get close
enough to the "Arena" to determine its exact function.
What is going on there needs to be investigated with
great urgency. The scale and frequency of the attacks
on the Punan are increasing, and amount to system-
atic genocide.*'

'What's genocide?' Jik asked.

'It's when people are killed because they belong
to a particular race or tribe,' Hanna told him.

'Like the Jews in Nazi Germany?' Ned said.

She nodded and put down the letter. She felt a desperate sense of disappointment. It told them little more than they knew already. She'd pinned so many hopes on Po's mystery package, and on other 'evidence' she was certain would be waiting for them at Blood River. Though she'd never defined exactly what form this evidence would take, she'd convinced herself that it would be important enough for them to be able to speed back to Sangabera with it, hand it over to the authorities and get Dad set free immediately.

She picked up the journal, flicked through it. As Po's letter had indicated, it was a list of victims' names, and the dates and places where they had been captured. She was astonished at how many there were. She looked for Felix's name—but of course, it wasn't there. The last entry had been written many days before he'd been kidnapped and flown to his death.

Mini shared her disappointment. The only new thing they'd learned was that the Arena was close to a mountain called Leopard Rock, which was somewhere in the Darma Range. Since they didn't know where either of these places were, it was not much help.

'Hanna! Mini! Come here! Look at this!'

Ned's excited voice made the girls glance up. He

and Jik had unfolded the map and were examining it closely.

They scrambled across and peered over their shoulders. A route had been marked on the map in black pen. It started near Blood River. Then it crossed the mountains, and snaked along a series of interlinked streams before ending up close to a triangular symbol indicating a mountain peak. Written next to it in Po's neat handwriting was the mountain's name: *Batu Kuli*—Leopard Rock!

Hanna felt a surge of excitement. Just when they were getting nowhere, the biggest breakthrough of all had happened! If they followed the map carefully, it would take them straight to the place where Felix had been killed—and straight to his murderer!

But how long would the journey take? Po had said it had taken him 'several' days. What on earth did that mean?

The map had a scale printed on its margin. Using it, they worked out that, even as the crow flies, Leopard Rock was over a hundred kilometres from Blood River. Mini estimated it would take eight or nine days hard jungle walking to get there.

Eight or nine days!

Hanna groped for the string in her pocket. There were only eight days left before Dad's execution! Even if they saved a day or two by walking as fast as they could, it would still leave them hardly any time to find Felix's real murderer and get him back to Sangabera.

Could they do it?

They had to try. Even if they were doomed to fail, they must give it their best shot. Besides, it wasn't just Dad they needed to save. It was Po and all the Punans who'd been captured with him. They would surely suffer the same fate as Felix unless they could be set free.

She leapt to her feet. 'Let's get going!' she said urgently to the others. 'Right now!'

22

The Riddle

Stopping only to fill up their bamboo water-carriers from a spring behind the hut, the four children and two dogs set off quickly in the direction Po's map indicated. The first part of their route followed the same path they'd taken earlier when they were searching for the bear's den. Sending the dogs out in front to sniff out danger, they ventured cautiously along it. Nobody wanted to meet a furious sun bear for the third time that day!

Fortunately, though Bahu and Leko picked up its scent, the animal was nowhere to be seen. As Jik said, it was no doubt curled up in its cave nursing a big dam headache!

It was soon clear that their journey would not be an easy one. Without warning, the path veered away from the river and began to climb steeply into the mountains. Gasping with the effort, wet with sweat, the children hauled themselves upwards for hour after hour.

Eventually they were forced to take a rest.

While they were getting their breath back,

Hanna noticed that Mini looked worried. She asked her what was the matter.

Mini made a helpless gesture. 'We've got no food! How can we get food when my blowpipe is broken and I cannot hunt? We will surely starve.'

'We can catch fish,' Hanna suggested. 'Jik's brilliant at fishing. He's got a net in his pack.'

'We're in the mountains. There are no fish up here.'

'There's always fruit,' Ned said cheerfully. 'We'll have to become vegetarians.'

Mini did not look impressed.

She was right to be concerned, Hanna knew. A long journey lay ahead of them. Without proper nourishment they would soon weaken, and might never reach their destination. But where could they find food in these barren mountains?

She found herself thinking about their warm, friendly kitchen back home in the cottage. Dad's special roast chicken would go down a treat right now—followed by one of Mum's gooey chocolate puddings. How she missed their life together!

The rest was a brief one. They knew they had to get as far into the mountains as possible before night fell. Then, somehow, they must find—or make—a shelter. At this altitude, temperatures could drop quite low before morning.

After a while Hanna took over the lead from

Jik. The path had begun to level off now, and was easier to follow. It was obviously regularly used. She was wondering who else would travel this way, when there was a sudden frenzy of barking, and half a dozen scruffy dogs charged out of the undergrowth and hurled themselves at Bahu and Leko.

A vicious dog-fight began. Bahu and Leko fought bravely, but were hopelessly outnumbered. Fur flew. Mini rushed to separate them. 'Be careful!' Hanna called out anxiously. If the dogs turned on her, she could be seriously hurt.

She needn't have worried. A loud hoot echoed through the forest. Instantly, the pack of dogs abandoned Bahu and Leko, and scurried off in the direction of the noise. Moments later, a figure emerged onto the path in front of them.

It was an old man. He was very short, very thin, and was naked except for a bark loincloth. A pair of pig's teeth hung from large holes in his earlobes. He was clutching a long, intricately carved blowpipe. A tiny monkey sat on his shoulder, chittering loudly, baring its fangs at the children.

Hanna, Ned, and Jik backed away, but Mini didn't share their alarm. 'I know this man,' she said reassuringly. 'His name is Asik. He is the grandfather of my Auntie Tama. He is very old, and lives in the forest in the traditional way. I think he can help us.'

She approached him, and spoke to him for a long time in the Punan language. Asik listened intently. The monkey eventually stopped being alarmed and started to groom the few remaining hairs on its master's almost bald head.

When Mini had finished, the old man replied in a strange, high-pitched voice. Hanna couldn't help noticing a strong odour coming from him—a mixture of unwashed skin and wood-smoke.

Mini turned to the others. 'Asik says he has seen these Leopard Men and they are very evil. They came to this place one time but did not take him away because he was too old. We can stay at his house tonight. He has food he can give us—pig meat and rice.'

'I thought Punan people didn't grow rice?' Ned asked, puzzled.

'We don't. The Kelabit and Kenyah people do. They give it to Asik.'

'Why do they do that?'

'He makes blowpipes—the very best blowpipes in the whole of Borneo. People travel for many days to obtain them from him. He does not like money, so they pay him with rice.'

'Cool!' exclaimed Jik.

Asik indicated that they should follow him. He

led them down a narrow track to his house, which was nearby. Like all the other Punan huts the children had seen, it was open-sided, raised from the ground on spindly poles, its roof thatched with broad forest leaves. Inside it, an old woman could be seen stirring something in a pot over a smoky fire.

Beyond the hut was a strange wooden contraption, lashed together with rattan strips. It looked like a kids' climbing frame.

And beyond that was a gigantic tree.

It had massive buttressed roots, and its upper branches disappeared into the dense forest canopy far above. But it had only half a trunk. The rest had been cut away in long vertical slices.

It was a *nyagang* tree, Mini explained. It gave the best wood of all for making blowpipes. The frame next to it held Asik's long iron drill, which he used for boring holes down their middle.

The old woman was Lawai, Asik's wife. She greeted them warmly as they climbed up the notched entrance pole into the hut. She had long, pierced earlobes and one of the jolliest faces the children had ever seen.

She also had pets.

Lots of pets.

There were two other monkeys in addition to the one on Asik's shoulder; a strange creature like

186

a big-eyed bush baby which was called a *ket* and lived in the rafters of the hut; numerous small singing birds in rattan cages; and a loud and extremely self-confident hornbill called Kwark. When several cats, and Asik's numerous hunting dogs were added to the mix, it was like being invited to spend the night in a zoo.

Lawai seemed genuinely delighted to see them, and immediately began to bustle about preparing food. Asik had killed a wild pig that morning, so there was plenty of meat for everyone.

While the food was cooking, the children attempted to explain their mission to the old man. It was difficult enough with Mini having to translate everything that was said into the Punan language, and back again. But Kwark made conversation virtually impossible. The hornbill obviously adored having guests, and spent his time leaping from one head to the next, making deafening 'kwark' noises directly into their ears. Eventually Lawai had to bribe him with a green banana to make him shut up.

Despite Mini's best efforts, Asik still seemed confused about where they were heading, and why. Trying to help, Ned unfolded Po's map and gave it to him. The old man examined it closely, then tapped it with his finger, and nodded. He called

Lawai across to him. She too tapped the map and nodded vigorously.

Had they spotted something important?

The children's hopes rose—only to collapse a moment later. The old couple had been looking at the map upside down!

They asked Asik about Leopard Rock. He knew of it, he told them. He'd even been there himself— just once, long ago, when he was a boy. He'd gone with his father to get medicine from a famous *day-ong*—a medicine man—who lived at the foot of the mountain. It was a very mysterious place. Very dangerous.

'Ask him what it looks like,' Ned said urgently.

The old man didn't reply to Mini's question. Instead, he got up, fished a piece of charcoal out of the fire, found a flat piece of wood, and began to draw on it.

A vivid landscape swiftly took shape. Rivers, waterfalls, and lofty jungle trees surrounded a broad, undulating plain, from the middle of which rose a strange, twin-peaked mountain. It looked like a giant thumb and forefinger pointing up to the sky. It was like no other mountain the children had ever seen. If the drawing was accurate, it would be impossible to mistake it when they saw it for real.

Asik was a brilliant artist. The picture was good

enough to be framed and hung in an exhibition. The children looked at him with fresh respect.

Then he said something that made Mini's eyes widen with surprise. 'He says that Leopard Rock is only four days' journey from this place.'

'That's impossible!' Jik said. 'We measured it on the map! It's more than one hundred dam kilometres. No way can we walk twenty-five kilometres in a day. It will take at least eight days to get there. Maybe more. You said so yourself!'

Mini questioned the old man again, convinced that she'd heard him wrongly. She hadn't. 'He says that from here it will take only four days to get to Leopard Rock, but eight days to come back again.'

'That's crazy!' Ned exclaimed. 'It doesn't make any sense at all.'

'It's a riddle. Punan people are very fond of riddles. He says he will tell us the answer in the morning. Now we must eat. The food is ready.'

23

Asik's Gift

Despite the snorts and squawks and snuffles of the animals, the tired children slept soundly. They were woken at first light by Lawai shuffling about, preparing breakfast, and packing up food for their journey. The remains of the wild pig, which had been smoking over the fire all night, were swiftly chopped into bite-sized pieces and packed into bamboo tubes, along with cooked rice and a handful of fiery chillies. A large bag of uncooked rice was added for later use. There was enough to feed a small army!

While the children were breakfasting, Asik disappeared beneath the house. He returned with a blowpipe.

It was the most beautiful blowpipe the children had ever seen, intricately carved, and polished to a glossy sheen. He presented it to Mini, along with a quiver of arrows.

The little girl was overwhelmed. 'This is an *upit mu'un*,' she said. 'The very best blowpipe of all! With it I can shoot very far and hit many things.'

She opened the quiver and carefully slid out an arrow. It had a sharp metal tip coated with poison. 'This is a *belat*. Until now I have never been permitted to use one. It can kill any animal in the forest, no matter how big!'

'That is so dam cool!' Jik said enviously. 'Can we have a blowpipe too?'

Mini asked Asik. He shook his head. 'He says it is too dangerous. But he has something even better to give you.'

The old man reached into a woven basket and took out four rattan bracelets. They were highly polished and etched with intricate designs. He gave one each to the children. 'Please, put them on,' Mini said. 'These are *jong*—dream bracelets. Asik carved them. If we wear them he will share our dreams. They will help to keep us safe from danger.'

Jik and Ned couldn't hide their disappointment as they slipped them onto their wrists. Somehow bracelets seemed so *girly*—blowpipes would have been much better!

Asik insisted on joining them for the first part of the journey. When they were ready, they said goodbye to Lawai, and set off northwards, accompanied by all the dogs, who seemed to have patched up their quarrel, and by Kwark who sailed along above everybody's heads croaking loudly.

Walking was much easier than the day before. By mid-morning they'd crossed the main mountain ridge, and were picking their way downhill on the far side. Every so often, a gap in the trees gave a panoramic view of the jungle below. It stretched away into the misty distance like an endless green sea. Here and there rivers glinted in the sunshine. To the children's disappointment, Leopard Rock was nowhere to be seen.

Though they asked him over and over again, Asik refused to tell them the answer to the previous night's riddle. Each time he gave a broad, toothless grin and shook his head. He was thoroughly enjoying the mystery, Hanna could see, and wanted to prolong the fun as much as possible.

At noon, they stopped to eat lunch beneath the shade of a large fig tree. Kwark spent the entire time stuffing himself with ripe fruit. The children were surprised he could still fly when the time came to get going again.

Shortly afterwards, without any warning, Asik led them off the main path onto a narrow track that dropped almost vertically downwards. There was the sound of rushing water. Moments later, they were picking their way along the boulders of a swift mountain stream. Other streams joined it, and before long it became a small river.

Eventually they arrived at a deep pool ringed with tall trees. Asik stopped, grinned, and muttered something in the Punan language. 'He says he will now solve the riddle,' Mini announced. 'Please watch carefully!'

At the rear of the pool was a pile of rocks. The old man rolled several of them away to reveal the entrance to a small cave. He reached inside and dragged something out.

It was a canoe.

It was black with age, carved from a single tree-trunk. It could seat three people—four at a pinch. Inside it were two sets of paddles.

Asik launched the little boat into the pool, where it bobbed merrily. Then he stood up, spread his hands proudly, and made a short speech.

Mini translated: 'He says that this is the answer to his riddle. This river flows fast, and has few rapids. If we take the canoe and paddle hard, we will reach Leopard's Rock in four days. Of course, if we want to paddle back again, *against* the current, it will take . . . '

'Eight days?' Ned suggested.

Mini glanced at him and grinned. 'Maybe even longer.'

Hanna's heart soared. 'Can we really borrow it?' she asked.

'It is a gift. He says he is too old to use it any

more, so it is now ours. He wishes us well on our dangerous journey.'

Hanna couldn't stop herself. She leapt across to Asik and hugged him. Because of his generosity, they would save four whole days—four days that could make the difference between life or death for Dad! It was the best answer to any riddle she'd ever heard. When she finally let him go, there were tears of happiness in the old man's eyes.

Asik held the canoe steady while they climbed in. It was a very tight squeeze. One thing was obvious: there was no way Bahu and Leko could fit in too. Reluctantly, Mini had to ask Asik if he would look after them for her. She'd return to fetch them at the first opportunity. Though the two dogs hated being left behind, and howled miserably, there was really no other solution.

Jik sat in the bow—he'd grown up with canoes like this back at the islands and was expert in handling them. Hanna was next; then Ned; and finally Mini. When they were all settled, Asik pushed them gently out from the bank. Instantly, the current caught them and whirled them away downstream. They managed a quick farewell wave.

As they sped along there was a familiar noise. Kwark was coming with them! He flapped alongside the canoe, croaking loudly, until they reached the first bend, when he suddenly lost his nerve and fled back to his master.

Now they really *were* on their own!

They took turns at paddling, propelling the little boat rapidly onwards. For a while the river remained open to the sky, but then the branches closed overhead, and they found themselves gliding through a green tunnel of leaves. It was a strange, dimly-lit world, noticeably cool after the heat of the sun, hung with mossy vines and lianas. Small, cross-looking turtles, perched on rocks, slipped silently into the water as the canoe passed. Kingfishers darted from branch to branch. A large deer, disturbed while drinking, crashed off into the undergrowth.

Anxious to check their progress, Hanna borrowed the map from Ned. Though it was quite detailed, she found it utterly impossible to read. There were no landmarks to guide her, and the entire sheet was criss-crossed with an intricate network of rivers and streams. It worried her for a minute or two, but then she realized it didn't matter. All the rivers were flowing in the same north-easterly direction, merging with each other as they went, before joining the mighty Barang and Kerai waterways. Whichever stream they followed should eventually bring them within sight of Leopard Rock.

Despite her cramped legs, and her dread of what was to come, Hanna felt a surge of optimism as they sped along. It was so nice not to be plodding down muddy, leech-infested jungle paths! The river was surprisingly smooth, with just a few minor obstructions. Only once were they forced to get out, to carry the canoe around a small waterfall.

Dusk came early in the deep shadow of the jungle trees. The boys proposed carrying on through the night, taking turns to rest. But Mini shook her head. It was too dangerous, she told them. Without proper lights they could easily hit a submerged rock, capsize, and drown. They must find a place to stop, soon.

A short time later, Jik spotted a deserted hut. It was tucked away up a small tributary stream, and was in surprisingly good condition. It occurred to Hanna later that it had probably been built by Asik himself, at exactly a day's journey from home, for use on his hunting expeditions.

The children soon got a fire going, and the rice and meat was put on to steam. The paddling had made them hungry, and everybody ate their fill.

After supper, they sat in silence, swatting at mosquitoes and watching the flickering firelight. They were all acutely aware that in the days to come they would need to be cleverer and braver than ever before if they were to have any hope of getting Po free and finding Felix's murderer. They were facing trained killers. It was possible—no, *probable*—that some of them—maybe all of them— would die.

'Does anybody want to call this whole thing off?' Hanna asked in a quiet voice. 'There's still time.'

Nobody did.

24

Jungle Lookout

For the next three days they propelled the canoe down a series of swift-flowing jungle rivers, each one a little wider and deeper than the last. They made camp on the riverbank each night, and set off again at the crack of dawn. On the fourth morning Mini spotted paw-prints leading past their sleeping platform down to the water's edge. They'd been visited by a leopard in the night! Luckily it can't have been hungry. Worried it might return with a better appetite, they packed their canoe quickly and fled.

The forest got denser with every hour that passed, pressing in from all sides, blocking out not just the light but—sometimes it seemed—the very air that they breathed. If their calculations were right, they must reach Leopard Rock soon.

But how would they know when they'd got there? The jungle was so thick they could easily paddle right by the mountain without realizing it.

Maybe they'd even passed it already!

There was only one answer. Somebody would have to climb up above the forest canopy to spot exactly where it was.

Jik volunteered immediately. He'd been climbing coconut trees on the islands back home since he was tiny, he told the others. He was so good at it, the other kids had nicknamed him *Amok,* which meant 'Monkey' in the Sea Gypsy language. A jungle giant would be no dam problem. To him, it was just a great big palm tree.

Not believing that it would be *quite* as easy as he said, the children steered the canoe into the bank, and climbed out. Using their *parangs*, they hacked their way into the forest.

It was like entering a land of giants. Something—the rainfall, or the fertility of the soil maybe—had produced the biggest trees they had ever seen. Their trunks soared skywards until lost from view in the dense canopy of greenery far above. If he felt scared at the thought of climbing one of them, Jik didn't show it. The only problem was deciding which to choose.

The tree he eventually selected was massive; and it was in trouble. Its trunk was wrapped inside the coils of a huge strangler fig. It was as if a monstrous wooden snake had gripped it and was slowly squeezing it to death. Eventually, Hanna knew, the fig would win the battle, and the tree would die and rot away, leaving just the fig's hollow framework to grow onwards and upwards.

But right now, the coils of the fig were as good as a ladder, giving solid footholds all the way up.

Without wasting any more time, Jik pulled off his trainers and began to climb.

He was very fast. Within minutes he was halfway to the top. No wonder his friends called him Monkey, Hanna thought admiringly, as he scrambled higher and higher. He could even teach an orang-utan a thing or two!

He looked no bigger than a tiny doll when he finally reached the thick curtain of greenery that marked the base of the canopy. He gave them a cheerful wave, and disappeared inside.

They might not be able to see him any longer, but the children could certainly *hear* where he had gone. An angry chorus of hoots, shouts, and whistles broke out as every creature in the canopy began to protest at the presence of an intruder. The gibbons sounded particularly furious, and Hanna became worried that Jik might be attacked. She was about to call up to him to tell him to be careful, when Ned stopped her. Human voices carried a long way in the jungle. It was vital they did nothing to give their presence away.

After a while the animals calmed down. They must have decided that a small boy with bare feet presented no danger to them. If only there were mobile phones in the jungle! Hanna would have given anything to find out exactly where Jik was, and what he could see.

He was gone a long time. Waiting below, the three children became increasingly anxious. What if something had happened to him high up in the branches? What if he *had* been attacked by a monkey—or worse, bitten by a snake? Ned had just volunteered to climb up after him when somebody dug Hanna in the ribs.

She whirled round in shock.

It was Jik!

He was standing right behind her, rocking with laughter. 'I give you a big dam surprise!' he chortled.

'Don't ever do that again!' Hanna scolded, her heart beating wildly. 'Where on earth did you come from?'

Jik pointed at a distant tree. 'I came down that one.'

'But how did you get over there?'

'I looked at the gibbons. They swing from branch to branch, tree to tree, no problem. So I did exactly like them—except I forgot which dam tree I came up in the first place, and climbed down the wrong one. Man, it's wicked up there! I saw an orang-utan with a baby. It was as close to me as I am to you right now!'

'Never mind the wildlife!' Ned said enviously. 'Could you see Leopard Rock?'

Jik nodded triumphantly. 'Very dam close to here!'

'How close?'

'Maybe two hours' walk.'

'Which direction?'

He waved his hand vaguely towards the east. 'I saw the Arena place too. It's built next to the bottom of the Rock.'

'Is it big?' Hanna asked.

'Massive!' He hesitated, for once lost for words. 'It's like . . . a football ground, a farm, and a prison, all mixed up together.'

'A *what*?' Ned demanded.

'I don't know how else to say it. There are very many dam people there. They are working in the fields, harvesting rice. Men with guns are guarding them.'

'Did you see Po?' Mini asked anxiously.

'Maybe, but I don't know what he looks like. When we get closer, you can see for yourself.'

Hanna was quivering with excitement. 'Shall we take the boat?'

Jik shook his head. 'From here it is better to

walk. There are many dam soldiers. Maybe they watch the river.'

The children hurried back to the canoe, dragged it out of the water and concealed it beneath leaves and fallen branches. Now for the final and most dangerous leg of their journey.

Next stop—Leopard Rock and the sinister Arena . . .

25

Familiar Faces

Jik took the lead. The best route to Leopard Rock was to follow the river for a while, he told the others, and then cut diagonally through the jungle towards it. The Rock was very tall, so it would be impossible to miss it once they were close enough. There must be complete silence from now on—there were armed men everywhere.

After a short while, the stream they were following joined a much bigger river. A wooden landing stage had been constructed where the two met. Tied up to it was a large longboat. Drums of fuel, sacks of cement, and a bundle of plastic drainage pipes were stacked nearby.

Guarding them was a sentry. He had a semi-automatic rifle slung over his shoulders, and was dressed in army uniform. The long, curved nail on the little finger of his left hand was clearly visible.

The children squirmed through the riverside vegetation to get a better view. The longboat looked familiar. It was the *Maidah*—Pak Mulut's boat, named after his mad wife—the same boat they'd travelled all the way from Sangabera in at the start of their journey. Its sharp-eyed owner must be visiting the Arena.

Did it mean that Dodi was there too?

The roar of an engine. A battered quad bike, pulling an empty trailer, bounced into view along a dusty track. It stopped next to the fuel drums, and its driver jumped down. It was Lucas, one of Pak Mulut's sons. The sentry ambled across to him. The two men lit cigarettes and chatted for a while. Then they began to load the building supplies and fuel onto the trailer.

While the men's attention was fixed on their task, the children left the river. Giving the landing stage a wide berth, they circled swiftly through the forest until they reached the track that the quad bike had just come down. They crossed it—Ned used a broken branch to brush away their footprints—and plunged into the secondary jungle beyond.

It was much harder to walk through than real jungle—full of tangled, thorny creepers. But there was no fear of getting lost. If they stayed close to the track, it would surely lead them directly to their destination.

Apart from a moment of panic when they heard the loaded quad bike returning from the jetty, and had to dive for cover, they made steady progress. It was late afternoon when Ned suddenly stopped and pointed upwards through a screen of trees. 'Look!' he said in an awed voice.

For some reason—perhaps because it was called a rock, and not a mountain—Hanna had imagined that Leopard Rock would be quite small.

It wasn't.

It soared vertically upwards, its twin peaks disappearing into a crown of swirling clouds. Here and there its sheer limestone walls were split into narrow fissures, allowing spindly plants to find a precarious foothold. A pair of white-headed eagles circled it, yelping mournfully. It had an air of brooding menace that made her shiver despite the intense heat.

Thrilled to see it at last, but disturbed by its looming presence, the four children hurried towards it.

After a while, the scrub began to thin. Dropping to their bellies, they wriggled forwards to check out what lay ahead.

They'd reached the edge of the rice fields which Jik had spotted from his lookout tree back in the jungle. They were dotted with stooping figures hard at work. Armed guards watched over them.

Beyond the fields, close to the base of the Rock,

was a complex of white-walled buildings surrounded by a high metal fence. Sentries with machine guns were stationed in watchtowers at each corner.

It had to be the Arena!

As she stared at it, Hanna felt her eyes mist with tears. She'd been thinking about this place—dreaming about it—for so many days now. Somewhere inside that forbidding compound was the heartless killer responsible for tearing her whole family apart.

Could they really hope to capture him and force a confession out of him in time to save Dad? They were just a bunch of kids after all.

But they were no ordinary kids, she told herself. The incredible adventures they'd already had together proved that.

She glanced at Ned, Jik, and Mini, sprawled flat on their bellies in the long grass, and felt a quiet confidence. Somehow—*somehow*—they could do it. She had no doubts at all.

But where to begin?

She turned her attention back to the Arena. For some reason she'd imagined that it would be lightly guarded—a place they could slip into unseen, do what they needed to do, and get out again fast. But it was more like a high-security prison.

There had to be a way past its defences, but

how could they find it? One false move and they would die in a hail of bullets. They needed to get a bird's-eye view of the entire complex, she decided. That way they could discover exactly what was going on inside, and check it out for any weak spots.

Short of a helicopter, there was only one way they could do that.

They must climb the Rock!

She was staring apprehensively at its forbidding limestone cliffs, when an excited squeak made her turn. Mini was pointing out across the fields. 'Po!' she exclaimed. 'I can see my Po!'

Hanna followed the direction of her finger. In the far distance, was a tall, thin white man with a beak-like nose. He looked like a friendly stork. He was dressed in a ragged shirt and shorts, and was wearing a conical hat to protect his head from the sun. He was harvesting rice, dropping the grain into a shallow basket hung from his neck.

'You're sure it's him?' Ned asked.

'Of course it's him!' Mini said frantically. 'Nobody else looks like my Po. I'm going to him. He needs me!'

She tried to get to her feet, but Jik pulled her down. 'Don't be crazy!' he hissed at her. 'Those guards will shoot you the minute they dam see you, and then they'll come looking for us!'

Mini struggled with him for a second or two. Then she stopped. 'I love him so much,' she said tearfully. 'He looks so unhappy.'

'We love our dad too,' Ned told her gently. 'We miss him just as much as you miss Po. But we'll get nowhere if we do daft things.'

Mini was silent for a while, blinking back her tears. Then she said, 'You're right. I'm sorry. I won't be silly like that again.'

Jik stretched out a hand to comfort her.

Speaking in soft whispers, Hanna outlined her plan to climb the Rock.

The boys were aghast. 'We'll be spotted straight away,' Jik said.

'Not if it's dark.'

'Are you seriously proposing that we climb that thing *at night*?' Ned spluttered.

'Why not? The moon will be up later. It'll give us enough light to see. I'll go on my own if you're scared.'

The boys looked at each other. 'We're not scared,' Jik protested.

'Nor am I,' Mini chimed in, anxious to make amends.

Hanna grinned. 'I thought that's what you'd say. Let's get as much rest as we can while we've got the chance. We're going to need all the strength we've got.'

26
Night Climb

The children got *some* rest, but not much. As the sun began to set, a siren sounded, and the men working in the fields—Po included—straightened up and began to shuffle slowly towards the Arena. Hanna wondered why they were walking so oddly. Then she saw that they were wearing leg-irons, like the ones she and Jik and Ned had been forced to put on back at the jungle airstrip. It must be so horrible working in them all day! Urged on by impatient guards, it took the exhausted men a long time to reach the main gates, which swung open as they approached.

To the children's surprise, the gates remained open after the last of the prisoners was inside.

They soon saw why.

An aircraft was approaching rapidly from the south, its paintwork gleaming in the light of the setting sun. It had twin engines, and looked very luxurious. Suddenly aware that they could be seen from above, the children swiftly covered themselves with grass and leaves, and lay with their faces pressed to the ground.

They needn't have worried. The plane came straight in, dropping down to land behind a fringe of trees on the far side of the farmland. Two Toyota Landcruisers, with darkened windows, sped out from the Arena to meet it.

They returned soon afterwards, and the gates closed behind them.

Whoever the new arrivals were, they were clearly very important.

The children used the last of the daylight to cover the final hundred metres or so to the foot of Leopard Rock. A small spring was trickling from a fissure. They took the opportunity to drink deeply from it, and to fill their bamboo water carriers.

Close-up, the Rock didn't look as difficult to climb as it had done from a distance. Its lower slopes were lined with thick bushes and creepers, which would provide excellent handholds. Further up, where the vegetation ended, a series of cracks and ledges snaked along its bare rock walls in more or less the direction they needed to go. Immediately above the Arena buildings was a narrow limestone overhang. From a distance it looked just wide enough to hold them all. If they could reach it, it would conceal them from prying eyes below, and give them a perfect view of the complex.

211

They finished off the previous evening's leftover rice. There wasn't very much of it, but it was too risky to light a fire and cook more. They would leave their packs and *parangs* behind, they decided. Carrying them would be too dangerous on the sheer rock face. Mini wanted to take her blowpipe with her, but was overruled. As darkness fell, they hid everything beneath a pile of boulders close to the spring, where it could easily be found when they returned.

The moon took an agonizingly long time to push itself above the eastern horizon, and when it did, its light was worryingly dim. A thin layer of cloud had covered the sky. It might brighten up later on, Hanna ventured, but nobody wanted to wait. They stood in silence for a moment or two at the bottom of the Rock, and stared up at its menacing bulk. 'Good luck everybody!' Ned whispered.

They began to climb.

The first part of the ascent was fairly easy. They hauled themselves swiftly upwards, using bushes and small outcrops of rock. The only problem came from hundreds of pitcher plants, which showered smelly water and decaying insects onto them as they pushed past.

But then the vegetation ended, and it got much harder.

The cracks and ledges they'd spotted from below were only just wide enough to provide a grip. But the main danger was from the limestone rock itself. It was soft and crumbly. Lumps of it broke away without warning and went crashing down into the bushes below. It would be a dead giveaway if anybody was patrolling nearby.

With their bodies pressed tight to the almost vertical walls, the children inched themselves towards the overhang. Progress was painfully slow—they were forced to test every toe and finger-hold before they dared trust it with their weight. Just one mistake would send them plunging to their deaths.

Jik, who was easily the best climber, took the lead, followed by Mini, then Ned and Hanna. As the minutes passed, the cloud cover thickened, and the moonlight disappeared completely. If it hadn't been for the glow of electric light from the buildings up ahead, it would have been impossible to continue.

The climb seemed to take for ever. As they approached the overhang, the lights from below grew brighter, leaving the children dangerously exposed on the bare rock-face. Anybody glancing up from below would have spotted them instantly.

Luckily, nobody did.

The last part of the ascent was by far the most difficult. The crack in the rock wall they'd been following ended just below the overhang. To get up to it, they would have to somehow traverse a smooth limestone slab that had no apparent hand-holds.

Was it possible? The thought of having to admit failure and return the way they'd come was more than Hanna could bear.

She reckoned without Jik.

Without saying a word, he slipped off his trainers and hung them round his neck. Then, using his bare feet, he began to push himself upwards.

It was one of the most extraordinary climbs Hanna had ever seen—even more impressive than the jungle tree. It was as if he had suckers attached to his hands and feet. Spiderman himself would have been envious!

After what seemed an age, but can have been only a minute at the most, Jik reached the edge of the overhang. He swung himself up onto it and disappeared from view. A large owl, which obviously used the place as a regular roost, flapped off silently into the night.

Now all the others had to do was follow him.

If only they had a rope!

Moments later Jik's face appeared over the lip of the overhang. He was holding the next best thing: a length of sinewy creeper. Was it strong enough to support their weight?

Jik wrapped one end of it round a rock, and threw the other end down to Ned. It was only just long enough.

Mini would go first, they decided. She was the smallest. She took a deep breath, grabbed the creeper, and scrambled upwards. Jik reached down and pulled her to safety.

Ned followed.

Then it was Hanna's turn.

She was the heaviest of the three. She'd almost reached the ledge when she felt the creeper begin to give way. She scrabbled desperately for a foot-hold to stop herself falling.

Miraculously, she found one.

But she was stuck. She couldn't go up or down. She could feel her strength fading. How much longer could she cling on?

'Grab hold of these!'

It was Ned's voice from above.

Glancing up, Hanna saw that the two boys had peeled off their T-shirts and tied them together. Lying flat on his stomach, with Jik and Mini holding onto his legs, Ned lowered them down to her.

She was just able to reach them. Gripping the shirts tightly, she fought her way upwards.

Seconds later she was hauled, gasping, on to the overhang.

At that precise instant, the generator, which had been powering the lights below, spluttered into silence, and the Rock was plunged into inky blackness.

27

Disaster

The overhang was quite narrow—only just wide enough to hold all four of them. The children spent a precarious night with their arms wrapped around each other, terrified of pitching over the edge in the darkness. As time went on, a thick mist rose up from the plain below and swirled around them, leaving them soaking wet and shivering. Hanna couldn't remember when she'd felt more miserable and exposed.

The mist was still there when dawn eventually broke. But as the sun rose higher, it began to thin. As soon as it was clear enough to see, the four children wriggled to the edge and peered downwards.

They had a perfect view. Spread out beneath them, enclosed by its sinister steel perimeter fence, was the entire Arena complex. It was much bigger than it had appeared from a distance. At its centre was a large, oval open space surrounded by wooden terracing, with floodlights at each end.

This was obviously the 'arena' that had given the place its name.

Facing on to it were two large buildings. One of them was a barracks—soldiers could clearly be seen moving about inside it. Opposite was another building of roughly the same size. This one looked much more luxurious, with a broad veranda overlooking the arena. Painted on the roof of the barracks in large letters were the words *PUSAT LATIHAN TENTERA HUTAN*. It meant 'Army Jungle Training Camp', Jik told the others. It was obviously intended to be read from the air.

Dotted around the complex were numerous smaller buildings joined up by neat brick paths. One of them was an open-sided kitchen. Other buildings were under construction. Sacks of cement, lengths of sawn timber, and bundles of plastic drainage pipes were dumped in several places across the site. The two Landcruisers, which had met the passengers from the plane the evening before, were parked near the main gate.

At first sight, the place really did look like a training camp. Soldiers—if they *were* soldiers— were emerging from the barracks and heading for a tin-roofed shed immediately beneath the overhang where the children lay. Judging by the smell and the splashing of water it was a toilet block.

But where was Po? Where were the captives

who'd shuffled in from the fields in chains the evening before?

Mini came up with the answer. 'Look!' she whispered furiously.

Away to the right, almost hidden by the leaves of a spreading tree, was a large cage. Like the perimeter fence, it was made from welded steel, interlaced with vicious-looking razor wire. It was crowded with men. Some were squatting. Others were standing, staring hopelessly out through the bars. Many of them looked sick; all of them were painfully thin. In one corner was a broken-down bamboo shed. Through its open door Hanna could see more prisoners stretched out on the bare earth.

Mini recognized many of the men. Some were from her own village, others she had met on hunting expeditions. They were all Punans. Moving amongst them, talking to them, obviously trying to keep their spirits up, was Po.

For one awful moment Hanna thought that Mini was going to call out to him. But to her relief, she stayed silent. She was shaking with rage. 'It is like a place for animals!' she hissed. 'No, worse than that! You wouldn't keep animals in that thing!'

As they watched, two armed soldiers came out of the barracks and crossed to the cage. It was time for work, Hanna guessed.

She was wrong. The soldiers called Po to the fence, and spoke to him briefly. Then they returned the way they had come. The prisoners, who had stood up when the soldiers had approached, sat down again. They looked relieved. Maybe they'd been given the day off.

Hanna turned her attention to the main perimeter fence, and began to examine it in detail. Her heart sank. There seemed to be no way in or out except through the heavily guarded main gates. Even if they had equipment to cut through the fence, they'd have no chance to use it. Any suspicious movement would be spotted immediately by the sentries in the watchtowers, and the penalty for being caught would surely be instant death.

But somehow they had to do it.

Somehow they had to get inside.

She turned to the others, but for once their ingenuity had deserted them. The best idea anybody could come up with was a suggestion from Jik that they went back to the jetty and hid inside an empty oil drum, in the hope that it would be loaded onto the quad bike and taken inside with the rest.

'It'll take too long,' Ned told him. 'And besides, I didn't see any empty drums when we were there.'

Jik confessed that he hadn't seen any either.

There had to be a solution! They must take note of everything that happened below, however unimportant it might seem. Something would suggest itself. It always did.

The sound of aircraft engines made them glance up sharply. The twin-engined plane they'd seen arriving the night before had taken off again. They froze as it circled the Rock, praying that they wouldn't be spotted; but the pilot's attention was obviously on his controls, and the plane headed swiftly south, disappearing from view.

They would take turns at keeping watch, they decided, after it had gone. That way they would all have a chance to catch up on some much-needed sleep. If anything important happened, the person on duty would wake the others up immediately.

Hanna volunteered to take the first one. Ned, Jik, and Mini didn't object and slumped gratefully back against the rock wall. Soon all three of them were asleep.

For a while nothing much happened. Then a movement on the veranda of the luxurious building next to the arena caught Hanna's eye. Cloths were being spread on tables by white-uniformed staff, plates and cutlery set out for breakfast. In the centre of each table was a small bunch of flowers. The place was obviously used as accommodation for guests. Hanna waited with interest to see who they might be.

A few minutes later a familiar figure emerged onto the veranda.

It was Dodi.

He looked different. He'd changed out of his T-shirt and jeans, and was now wearing a smart police uniform.

He inspected the tables; spoke sharply to one of the servants, who scurried to fetch a piece of missing cutlery. Then, seemingly satisfied, he stopped, stretched, and stared up at Leopard Rock.

Hanna withdrew her head quickly. When she dared look again, he had gone.

The smell of cooking rose up into her nostrils. Something delicious was being prepared in the kitchen. Trying to ignore her hunger, she forced herself to concentrate on the breakfast area. Whoever the diners were, they must surely soon come out to eat.

They did.

She counted nine of them. All were men. They were dressed, for the most part, in lightweight safari suits. Most were middle-aged or older.

They were chatting familiarly with each other, sharing jokes as they took their seats. They reminded Hanna of her boring Uncle Robin and his friends at the golf club back home. What on earth were these people doing here in the middle of the jungle, she wondered? Was it some sort of posh hunting trip? It was the only thing she could think of.

Then a tenth man emerged.

He was quite old, with closely-cropped white hair. There was something familiar about his face. Hanna stared at him for a moment, puzzled. Then her stomach contracted with shock.

It was the judge who'd condemned Dad to death!

His grim features were unmistakable.

She woke the others, who crowded to the edge of the overhang to take a look. They were as astonished as she was. What on earth was he doing here, so far from his courtroom in Sangabera? Was he somehow involved in Felix's death? It scarcely seemed possible.

A waiter came across and offered the judge a bread roll. As he took one, the children saw that his fingernail was curved into a sharp-pointed claw.

The mystery had just got deeper.

The diners took their time over breakfast. When they had finally finished, Dodi came out from the guest house again. He was carrying a clipboard. He spoke to each of the visitors in turn, and noted down their replies. He was charming and attentive, listening carefully to everything that was said. He reminded Hanna of a holiday rep, organizing the day's activities. Though they tried desperately to hear what was being said, it was too far for sound to carry.

Eventually everybody went inside, and the tables were cleared. Soon afterwards, a squad of soldiers emerged from the barracks carrying sections of wooden staging. A platform was set up in the arena next to the guest house. Other soldiers strung lines of coloured electric lights between the surrounding buildings. Clearly, some sort of ceremony was about to take place.

Towards noon, the twin-engined aircraft returned. The Landcruisers went to meet it at the airstrip and brought back more visitors, who were greeted by Dodi at the entrance to the guest house and escorted inside. Once again they were all men. They seemed hugely excited, joking and laughing loudly as they went. Most of them had claw-like fingernails.

The children tried to catch up on more sleep, but it was impossible. As the sun rose higher, the heat on the exposed overhang became almost unbearable. What little water they had left was nearly gone. One thing was clear: they couldn't spend much longer where they were. They would die of thirst or heatstroke. The thought of retracing their steps along the crumbling cliff face made Hanna shiver with dread.

Work continued in the arena well into the afternoon. Wooden poles, festooned with brightly-coloured strips of bark, were positioned at intervals around its edge. But it was what was happening in its centre that intrigued the children most.

A large wooden carving of an animal was carried in and positioned in front of the platform. Its paint was faded, and it was chipped and dented as if it had been struck many times with something sharp—an axe, maybe. At first Hanna thought it was some kind of imaginary beast. But then she realized that it was a crouching leopard, with evil, human-like eyes, flared nostrils, and rows of jagged, white teeth.

Was it just for decoration, or did it have some other, more sinister purpose? Whatever it was for, she found it strangely disturbing, and tried not to look at it.

The soldiers who had brought the carving in bowed their heads to it respectfully, and went away. Soon after that, the doors of the guest house opened, and the visitors came out. They, too, bowed their heads to the leopard statue. After pausing to admire the decorations, they followed Dodi to the cage that held the Punans.

They clustered in front of it, peering intently inside, pointing out things to each other, making comments. They reminded Hanna of visitors to a zoo. Po said something to them angrily, but was ignored. They seemed to be making some sort of selection; comparing notes. Dodi wrote down their choices on his clipboard. It took quite a long time, but eventually they all seemed satisfied, and followed him back to the guest house.

As they did so, another plane came in to land at the airstrip. This time it was the small, green Cessna. One of the Landcruisers went out to meet it. When it returned, two people got out. One was the American pilot. The other was a woman. She was wearing a long, hooded garment that concealed her face. The two new arrivals hurried inside the guest house and the doors closed firmly behind them.

'Well?' Ned said in a disappointed voice.

'Well what?' Hanna asked.

'Haven't we seen enough? Has anybody got any fresh ideas about how we're going to get inside that place and get out again without being caught?'

Nobody had.

'We need a dam helicopter,' Jik said.

'Well we haven't got one,' Ned snapped. 'And even if we had they'd shoot it down!'

'If only it was a normal day,' Hanna said, as frustrated as her brother.

'What do you mean by that?' he demanded.

'If it was a normal day they'd be following a routine and we could get to know what it was. We could identify any weak spots.'

'They don't have any weak spots!' Ned said bitterly. 'Even the SAS couldn't get into that place without a massive firefight.'

'We can't just give up!' Jik exclaimed. 'One of those men down there murdered Felix. We can't just give up and go away!'

'I will never give up,' Mini announced stoutly. 'Not until I've got my Po back!'

'So what in God's name do we do?' Ned aimed a frustrated kick at a nearby lump of rock.

He regretted it instantly.

As if in slow motion, the rock—the size of a small football—broke away from the cliff-face and sailed into space. The children watched in horror as it plunged downwards. It hit a ledge, bounced twice, leapt the fence, and crashed onto the metal roof of the toilet block below.

28

An Old Enemy

If a bomb had gone off, it couldn't have made much more noise. A soldier staggered out of the toilet, his trousers still round his ankles. He was shouting wildly, pointing upwards at the overhang. Alarm bells shrilled. Soldiers began to pour out of the barracks, grabbing their weapons as they did so.

The children flung themselves flat, but there was nowhere to hide. As if in a dream, Hanna watched as one of the soldiers raised his gun and fired.

Bullets whined off the surrounding rocks. Jik let out a sharp yelp of pain. Blood was trickling from his forehead. For one horrible moment Hanna thought he'd been hit; but it was just a scratch from a flying fragment of rock.

More shots rang out. This time they were aimed too low—but it was just a matter of time before somebody hit the target.

There was a sudden shout. The gunfire stopped immediately. An overweight man in an army uniform waddled quickly out of the guest house.

Judging by the collection of gold stars on his shoulder-tabs he was a general. He was followed closely by Dodi.

They joined the group of soldiers near the toilet block who were staring up at the children. Amongst them Hanna spotted the familiar, sharp-eyed features of Pak Mulut.

Escape was impossible. The four children stood up slowly, with their hands raised.

The general bellowed at them in Indonesian, indicating that they should come down immediately. Hanna stepped forward gingerly and peered over the edge of the overhang. It was a sheer drop of many metres to the ground below. There was no way they could obey his order without falling to their deaths. Even the route they'd used to climb up the night before looked impossible in daylight—especially with a dozen guns pointed at your back.

'We're stuck!' she yelled down. 'We can't move!'

The general went red in the face, furious that his order was being disobeyed. He looked as if he might explode at any moment. Dodi approached him and said something into his ear.

It had an immediate effect. The general nodded, turned, issued a sharp order. A short while later a squad of soldiers emerged from the barracks carrying ropes and harnesses. One of them had a loudhailer which he handed to Dodi.

The detective's amplified voice boomed up to the children from below. 'Stay where you are! Do not move, and do not try to escape! You will be rescued!'

They had no intention of going anywhere.

There was a small gate in the perimeter fence. It gave access to the base of the Rock. Bolts were slid back, and the soldiers carrying the mountaineering equipment hurried through. This section of the Rock must have been used for climbing practice in the past, Hanna realized, because steel pitons were already hammered into the cliff face. She was furious with herself for not having spotted them earlier—or the gate. Maybe—just maybe—they could have climbed down and got inside the fence without being seen.

But maybes didn't matter any more . . .

One of the soldiers clambered rapidly up towards them, trailing ropes. He reached the overhang and swung himself onto it. Ignoring the children, he hammered a piton into the rock, tested it for grip and anchored the ropes to it.

Then he turned, unclipped a harness from his belt and put it on Ned. He was to go first.

Ned had been on a climbing course in Wales with his school, and knew what to do. Determined to prove he was not afraid, he swung himself over the edge and abseiled swiftly down.

At the bottom a soldier grabbed him and marched him away.

Jik went next.

Then it was Mini's turn.

She was about to climb into the harness when a furious bellow stopped her.

It was Po! He'd seen what was happening and had rushed to the side of his cage.

Their eyes met. '*Po!*' Mini screamed, tears wetting her face. '*Po, it's me!*' She fought wildly with the soldier who was trying to strap her in.

Po hurled himself against the bars. 'Take your hands off that girl!' he yelled, his face distorted with rage. 'Touch her and you're dead!'

He was joined by the rest of the prisoners. They too were shouting at the tops of their voices.

A whistle shrilled. A detachment of soldiers raced out of the barracks. They were carrying clubs and whips.

They stormed into the cage. Blows rained down on unprotected heads, arms, and shoulders. Po tried to fight back, but he was clubbed to the ground.

There was a second whistle blast, and the soldiers left as quickly as they had come, leaving piles of groaning, writhing bodies behind them.

Mini was hysterical with rage and shock. The soldier on the overhang tried to get her into the harness once again, but she fought with him. For one terrifying moment the pair of them teetered close to the edge of the overhang, and Hanna thought they were going to fall.

A punch landed. Half-stunned, Mini was finally lowered to the ground. Protesting loudly, Hanna was sent down after her.

They were hustled inside the compound, and the gate was closed. Mini was starting to struggle again. Dodi strode up to her, jerked up her chin, then let it drop. 'She's a Punan,' he said contemptuously. 'Put her with the others. They might as well say their last goodbyes to each other!'

Still struggling, she was dragged away. The cage door clanged shut behind her.

What did the detective mean by *'their last goodbyes'*, Hanna wondered? The remark must have been aimed at her and Ned, or he wouldn't have used English. She felt a sudden burst of fear. Something told her they were about to find out why nobody ever came back alive from Leopard Rock.

They were frog-marched rapidly into the arena. Dodi and the general, who were leading the way, bowed their heads to the leopard statue as they passed. Close up it looked even more scary than it had done from a distance. Something dark stained its flanks. Could it be congealed blood? Without slackening their pace, the three children were thrust inside the guest house and the door slammed shut behind them.

As their eyes adjusted to the gloom, they stared around themselves in amazement. The room they found themselves in was like the one in Pak Mulut's house back in Long Gia, only much bigger and far more splendid.

Spears, shields, swords, and richly-decorated headdresses festooned with hornbill feathers and intricate coloured beadwork occupied every square centimetre of wall space. Deer antlers and bear-skins were nailed to the doors. There was even a rhinoceros head mounted on a polished wooden plaque.

Hanging from the ceiling on stout chains was a massive war canoe. It was at least twelve metres long, made from carved and painted wood. Intricately carved paddles were ranged along its sides, giving it a strange resemblance to a Viking longship.

They scarcely had time to take it all in before a door at the far end of the room opened, and a bizarre procession entered.

It was the visitors who'd flown in over the past two days—amongst them, the judge. They'd abandoned their western clothes and were now dressed as Kenyah warriors, with feathered headdresses, animal skin capes, and red loin-cloths. Most of them were clutching spears and shields.

They should have looked scary, but they didn't. Maybe it was because of their knobbly-knees and pot-bellies—or the fact that several of them were still wearing their watches. They reminded Hanna of the people back home in England who dressed up as Roman soldiers at the weekends and had pretend battles. If things hadn't been so serious, she would have laughed out loud.

Could this place be some kind of theme park—a jungle Disneyland for adults—she wondered? She glanced at the boys. They looked as puzzled as she was.

A carved wooden chair, draped with a richly-woven cloth, stood on a low dais at the far end of the room. It had handles to allow it to be carried, Hanna noticed. The 'warriors' went up to it and ranged themselves in a semi-circle behind it, as if it was a throne. They were glancing expectantly at the door they had just come through.

For several long minutes, nothing happened. Then it creaked slowly open, and a figure entered.

It was a woman. Because of the gloom it was impossible to see her face clearly. She was wearing a blood-red floor-length robe, over which was draped the skin of a rare clouded leopard.

On her head was a spectacular headdress of black and white hornbill feathers, decorated with vividly-coloured beadwork and what looked like tufts of human hair. Large, carved bone earrings dangled on either side of her cheeks.

Whilst the men looked silly in their costumes, this newcomer certainly didn't. The three children watched in awe and fear as she glided silently across to the 'throne' and sat down.

As she did so, a shaft of sunlight, shining in through a high window, lit up her face.

They gasped in astonishment.

Was it?

Could it be?

It was only when she turned towards them and began to speak, that they knew for certain.

It was the Datin—wife of the evil Datuk Kamal—whom they'd last seen being taken away by police at the end of their terrifying adventure on Shark Island . . .

29

The Brotherhood of the Claw

'Welcome to Leopard Rock,' the Datin said softly. 'You're a little late, but who cares about that! Please, come closer.'

Dodi ushered the astonished children across to the throne. The Datin was as beautiful as ever. With her high cheekbones and almond-shaped eyes, and the extraordinary headdress she wore, she could have been a top Parisian catwalk model showing off the latest fashion extravaganza.

Hanna couldn't stop herself: 'I thought you were in prison!' she blurted out.

The Datin smiled. 'I did spend a few days in jail, Hanna, but it was *so* unpleasant I decided to make other arrangements.'

'What other arrangements?'

'I was given time off for good behaviour and released.'

'After only a few days?'

The Datin shrugged. 'Anything can be "arranged" when you have friends in high places.

And I have them in the highest places of all. Isn't that true, Your Excellency?'

She turned to one of her 'attendants', a small man in an oversized headdress, clutching a spear and shield. Hanna recognized him vaguely from news broadcasts back home. He nodded in agreement.

The Datin swung back to the children. As she did so, Hanna noticed her hands. All ten of her fingernails were curved into sharp-pointed claws and painted blood-red to match the colour of her robe. 'I'm so glad you're in time to take part in our festival tonight! We're going to have so much fun!'

'What sort of fun?' Ned asked, finding his voice at last.

The smile again. It was like a leopard contemplating its prey. 'It would spoil it if I told you, Ned. You'll find out soon enough. Dodi was concerned that you wouldn't make it here in time for our festival. But I told him not to worry. I knew you would turn up. I told him that you are the bravest, cleverest children I've ever come across, and we all like brave children, don't we, gentlemen?'

Her attendants nodded vigorously. 'Yes, yes!' one of them said loudly in English.

'Why is it so good we're brave?' Ned asked, mystified. 'Would it make any difference if we were cowards?'

The Datin looked shocked. 'Oh yes! You would be useless for our purpose—quite useless!'

'How did you *know* we were going to turn up here?' Hanna said.

'Because I arranged that as well.'

'I don't believe you!'

The Datin's eyes narrowed. She didn't like being challenged. 'I have arranged everything, right from the very beginning. You have destroyed my family. My husband the Datuk—or should I call him the Sea Wolf—has not recovered from the injuries he received the last time you met, and now spends part of his time in a wheelchair. My children have serious behavioural problems and are on medication. We have lost nearly all our money. But most importantly, we have lost face. Do you know what losing face means?'

Hanna shook her head.

'We have been humiliated. Publicly humiliated. And that can never be forgiven or forgotten. It was impossible to take my revenge on you while you were in England. But when I heard that your father had come to Borneo on a fool's errand to find gold, it gave me the perfect opportunity. So I arranged to have him arrested and sentenced to death.'

'You *arranged* it?'

'With a little help from His Honour, here.' She

indicated the judge. 'He is the Datuk's brother, by the way, and is as furious as I am about what has happened.

'The rest was simple. You're such a very close family, I knew that the first thing you would all do when you heard of your father's plight would be to fly out to Borneo. Dodi took care of the rest: the disturbance in the courtroom; your mother's detention; your boat-ride upriver. Of course you weren't meant to escape—those fire ants were a brilliant idea, by the way—but I was thrilled when you did! More proof of your bravery! They'll be here soon, I kept telling Dodi. Nothing will stop those children. And I was right. All the clues that were left for you led you right here. You have been—how shall I put it—puppets on a string, dancing to my tune. And believe me, there'll be lots more dancing tonight!'

'What *is* this dam place?' It was Jik who spoke.

The Datin turned towards him. 'Ah, the Sea Gypsy boy! I had heard you were in England with the others. Your people helped to destroy my family every bit as much as Ned and Hanna, so I am delighted you can join us. This place is . . . '

She paused, turned to her attendants. 'What would you say this place is, gentlemen?'

'Paradise?' one of them ventured. There was laughter.

The Datin smiled. 'Not quite, but I'm very flat-tered. This place is . . . somewhere where very important people from all over Asia can come to regain their lost youth and strength.'

'You mean it's a *health spa*?' Ned asked.

More laughter. Hanna glared at the Datin. She hated Ned being made an object of amusement. 'It's an army camp,' she snapped. 'It says so on the roof!'

'Of course. And we can prove that if anybody asks. But this is an army camp with a difference. Everybody here—even the lowest cook in the cook-house—is a member of the Brotherhood.'

'What Brotherhood?'

The Datin looked surprised. 'I thought you might have worked that out already! We are the Brotherhood of the Claw, one of the most feared and powerful secret societies on this planet. We have existed almost as long as Borneo itself, and I am its elected queen!'

'Why are you telling us all this?' Hanna chal-lenged. 'Aren't you afraid we might give your secret away?'

Yet again there was laughter from the assem-bled men—one of whom, Hanna noticed, was the American pilot.

The Datin joined in the laughter. 'No, Hanna, there is no possibility of that. None whatsoever!'

She looked as if she was going to say more, but stopped herself. She glanced up sharply at Dodi. 'I must rest—it is going to be a long night. I've had enough of these children and their questions for now. Put them somewhere until they are needed.'

'Where, your majesty?'

A slow smile crossed the Datin's face. 'How about the Death House? That will be rather . . . *amusing.*'

30

The Death House

What was happening? What did it all mean? Unanswered questions pounded at Hanna's brain. One thing was certain: she wasn't as brave as the Datin thought she was—nor, judging by their ashen faces, were Ned and Jik.

Sure, they'd been brave up to now. But there'd always been hope—hope that they'd discover the truth; hope that they'd get Dad free; hope that they'd soon all be back together again, as happy as they'd been before this whole nightmare had started.

But now that hope was gone, and its place had been filled by black despair. There was to be no escape from Leopard Rock, nor from the evil woman who controlled it. She was like a spider, and they were like flies caught in her web. The more they struggled, the more they became trapped.

Dusk was falling as they were dragged outside. A generator had started up and lights were beginning to flick on—first, the strings of multicoloured bulbs, then the powerful floodlights, lighting up the arena like day.

Final preparations for the evening's festivities were under way. Fires had been lit outside the cookhouse, and whole pigs were being roasted. Vast vats of rice were bubbling and steaming. Hanna spotted Pak Mulut ferrying crates of whisky and beer across to the guest house on the quad bike. He too was now dressed as a Kenyah warrior. As they passed, their eyes met, but his face stayed blank. It was as if they had never met before. There was no sound from the cage where Po, Mini, and the Punans were being held.

The children were taken to the far end of the arena. Filling most of the available space was a large hut made from solid jungle wood. It was painted all over with intricate, swirling patterns in black, white, and red, featuring strange horned faces with staring eyes and protruding tongues. It reminded Hanna of the spooky Kenyah tombs they'd seen on their way upriver. The words *Rumah Mati* were written above its door.

It was the Death House.

The children were bundled inside, and the door locked behind them.

At first, the darkness seemed total. But then Hanna realized that there were windows of a sort—narrow slits in the wooden walls, giving a limited view of the arena. There was a strange, unpleasant smell—a mixture of smoke and strong chemicals, like the sort you pour down the toilet. She wondered where it was coming from.

Ned provided the answer. 'Look,' he said in a quavering voice.

He was pointing upwards at the rafters.

Hanging from them were dozens of what, at first sight, looked like footballs in net bags.

They weren't.

They were heads—*human heads*—cut off at the neck, and bound with rattan cords.

Some looked ancient—shrunken and black—with gaping eye-sockets and bared teeth.

But many seemed more recent, the flesh on their skulls fresh and plump, their lips pouting and full.

Hanna let out a scream of horror.

It was met by a peal of laughter from outside. It was Dodi. He must have been been waiting to hear their reaction, to convey it to the Datin. 'Enjoy your stay in the Death House!' he called out to them as his footsteps retreated.

Hanna struggled to control herself. She wanted to scream and keep on screaming. But she must stay strong for the boys' sake. If she caved in now, everything would be lost.

Ned was still staring at the severed heads, his

body rigid with shock. Jik was huddled against one of the wooden posts that supported the roof, muttering loudly to himself. He was repeating the word *'saitan!'* over and over again.

He was talking to the evil spirits he believed existed in graveyards and places where people had died, Hanna knew—no doubt begging them for mercy. Despite his time in England and America he was still a Sea Gypsy at heart, and always would be. She crossed towards him. He was at breaking-point, she could tell. 'Jik, listen to me!' she said urgently.

'Hanna?'

It was Ned's voice. He was pointing fearfully at the rafters.

'Don't look at them!' she snapped, turning her attention back to Jik.

'But they're moving! The heads are moving, Hanna!'

She followed his gaze. As she watched, the nearest head swung slowly towards her. Its lips—or what remained of its lips—were pulled back over its gums, revealing a double row of gleaming white teeth. It was smiling at her. It was going to speak . . .

Of course it isn't, she told herself desperately. *Control yourself! It's just a head. Just part of a dead body. It's just*—she groped for the right words—*just a lump of dried meat!*

245

The other heads were moving now, twisting and spinning in their rattan slings. Any moment now they would burst out laughing, she became convinced of it. Somewhere inside herself she could already hear the high-pitched cackle of their ghostly voices.

A terrified whimper made her turn. Jik had gripped the wooden post next to him and was pulling himself to his feet.

Suddenly she understood: it was Jik making the heads dance! His slightest movement was making them bob up and down as if strung on elastic.

She crossed to him quickly, unwound his arms from the post, and led him back to Ned. The heads continued to twist and turn for a moment or two, then, thankfully, they became still. The three children sat down together on the floor. Both boys were sobbing. 'Stop it!' Hanna said to them, sounding much sterner than she felt. 'We've got to be brave, otherwise there's no hope for us!'

'There *isn't* any hope,' Ned told her through his tears. 'And we don't have to be brave. We're going to be killed whatever happens.'

'No we're not!'

'Yes we are!' He pointed wildly up at the roof. 'Our heads are going to be hung up there—yours and mine and Jik's. And so are Mini's and Po's and all the other Punans'. Because these people are *head-hunters*! Don't you understand that?'

'Don't be stupid!'

'It's not me that's being stupid!'

Hanna sucked in a deep breath. Despite her protestations, she knew that he was right. How else could the gruesome collection swinging from the rafters be explained?

She knew all about head-hunting, of course. It featured in every book she and Ned had ever read about Borneo. In the old days, the heads of enemies killed in battle or in ambush were cut off by the victors and brought back to the tribal village to be preserved and displayed. They brought power and prestige to the whole tribe—especially to the warriors who'd done the killing. They believed that their victims' bravery and strength would be added to their own, and that the more heads they cut off, the stronger and braver they would become, until eventually they could never be defeated in battle, and would never grow old.

But head-hunting had been banned for well over a hundred years. Could it *really* still be going on?

A remark the Datin had made to them came back to her—about important people coming to Leopard Rock 'to find their lost youth and strength'.

Ned had thought she'd meant it was a health spa!

But what if it was more sinister than that?

What if all those old, fat, knock-kneed men in their silly costumes really *did* believe they could get their youth and strength back if they cut off people's heads? And that the more heads they cut off, the younger and stronger they would become?

It was a crazy idea! Utterly preposterous. This was the twenty-first century. Nobody believed in that kind of rubbish any more.

Or did they?

Suddenly, sickeningly, the final pieces of the jigsaw began to fall into place. If it was true, it would explain the Leopard Men and their kidnapping raids. Their victims—the Punan—were hunter-gatherers, living deep in the forest. Nobody knew how many of them there were, and there was nobody—apart from their families—to miss them when they disappeared. After they'd been captured they were brought to Leopard Rock, like cattle to a slaughter-house, and kept alive in a cage until the time came for their heads to be hacked from their bodies. It was why none of them were ever seen again.

It would account for the myth of the *bali saleng* too. If local people believed that there were demon blood-collectors roaming the forest, they would stay well away, and there would be no risk that anybody would accidentally stumble across what was going on.

And it would explain what had happened to Felix. She remembered Dodi saying that parts of his corpse were *missing* when it was found.

One of those parts must have been his head.

Felix was as strong as an ox, and twice as brave. Whoever had been chosen to strike the final blow must have felt as if they'd won the lottery! Maybe it had even been the Datin herself. She was blood-thirsty enough, and it would have fitted in perfectly with her evil plans for revenge.

Felix's severed skull was probably hanging somewhere in this very hut! Hanna kept her eyes firmly focused on the floor. If it was up there, she didn't want to see it.

There could be no doubt now: the Brotherhood of the Claw was a gang of very posh, very rich, very ruthless modern-day head-hunters.

And she and Ned and Jik were going to be its next victims.

It was why Dodi had brought them upriver in the first place.

It was why their lives had been spared up to now.

And it was why the Datin had been more than

willing to tell them all her secrets—knowing they'd never have a chance to give them away.

Hanna fumbled in her pocket. There were just two knots left on her piece of string—two days before the firing squad in Sangabera pointed their rifles at Dad's heart and pulled the triggers.

The Datin had won. Her revenge was complete.

In two days' time Mum would be a widow, and her children would be dead.

31

In the Arena

The three children huddled together in the centre of the floor. There was nothing more to be said; nothing more to be done. Hanna could feel the hot tears trickling down her cheeks. Would it hurt, she wondered? Would there be pain when the final blow landed? Or would death come so quickly there'd be no time to feel anything?

She remembered Pak Mulut's sword, the one he'd shown them back at his house in Long Gia. What was it called? A *mandau*? It had looked very sharp. With a sword like that, death would be instant. Just one cut.

But what if the sword they used wasn't sharp? What if it took more than one blow? Those old men didn't look very strong. What if they just kept hacking away, injuring you without killing you? What if you went on living for a while after your head was cut off? What if you ran about like a headless chicken? What if . . .

Hanna's panic was turning into blind hysteria— but it didn't matter. As Ned had said, there was no more need to control yourself. No more need to be brave.

Except there was! Her own pride was at stake; her own self-belief. She was *not* a coward—and she refused to become one! If bravery was what these killers wanted from her they could have it in bucketfuls. See if she cared!

She took a deep breath—and another—willing her racing heart to slow. Outside, music had started up: the thud of bamboo drums, the clang of brass gongs, the shriek of wooden flutes, amplified through numerous speakers. Untangling herself from the boys, she stood up and crossed to the slatted window.

It was night now, and the arena was brilliantly floodlit against the surrounding blackness. Banks of seats were filling up rapidly with excited spectators, all dressed as Kenyah warriors. For a moment Hanna was puzzled. Where had all these new people come from? Then she realized: they were soldiers. They'd swapped their uniforms for loincloths and hornbill-feather headdresses.

Food was being passed around—pork and rice wrapped in banana-leaf packets. It smelt delicious. Hanna's empty stomach knotted with hunger. It was more than twenty-four hours since they'd eaten anything.

Drink was circulating too—bottles full of clear

liquid that could only be *arak*. Already some of the men were showing signs of drunkenness.

She felt Ned press up beside her—then Jik. Curiosity had overcome their fear. As all three of them peered out, the music got suddenly louder, and two men in full warrior gear leapt into the arena. They were carrying swords and shields.

They walked about casually for a moment or two, as if neither was aware of the other's presence, their brilliantly-polished swords glinting in the bright lights. Then, their eyes met. Instantly they dropped to a crouch, peering at each other from behind their shields. As the drums pounded, they began to circle round, searching for an opening. Was it a real fight, or some kind of complicated dance? Hanna couldn't be sure.

After a short while, one of them leapt to his feet and rushed at his opponent. The other sidestepped instantly and, to the roars of the crowd, a high-speed swordfight began. The fighters jumped and twirled, the polished steel of their weapons flashing. It looked certain that one or both of them must soon be seriously injured; but they weren't.

The contest ended when one of the swordsmen deftly tripped his opponent, who landed on his back, his sword flying out of his hand. The victor leapt onto his chest and pretended to saw off his head. Then, ripping off his headdress, he raced round the arena to the roar of the crowd, punching the air like a footballer who'd just scored a goal.

A second swordfight followed immediately—then a third—the spectators roaring their support for their chosen favourites. Money was changing hands as the increasingly drunken 'warriors' took bets on the outcome. Hanna felt a tiny glimmer of hope. *Nobody was being killed.* Was the whole thing some kind of elaborate set-up, like those American wrestling matches, where the fighters pretend to break each other's backs, but really don't?

She was about to ask the boys what they thought when Jik suddenly pointed at something through the window.

Hurrying towards the Death Hut, dodging drunken spectators, was a familiar figure. It was Pak Mulut, wearing full Kenyah costume. He was clutching packets of pork and rice, and a bottle of drinking water. Using a key from a large bunch, he swiftly unlocked the door, and thrust the food and drink into the children's hands. 'Eat,' he said urgently. 'Get strong!' Then he slammed the door shut, locked it again, and was gone.

The children exchanged astonished glances. Why had he bothered to bring them food? Surely, if they were going to die it didn't matter whether they ate or not.

Then Hanna remembered: the last time Pak Mulut had given them food and urged them to eat, was just before they'd been abandoned on the riverbank. Was something similar going to happen this time? Something they didn't know about, but which they would need every bit of their strength to survive?

One thing was certain: whatever it meant, it didn't alter the fact that they were starving! Opening their packets, they tucked in hungrily. The food was delicious, and the water—they were relieved it wasn't *arak*—tasted brilliant too. Even before they'd finished their feast, they could feel some of their old optimism returning.

The sword contests continued for a short while longer, the roars and cheers from the spectators getting louder and more raucous by the minute.

Then, without warning, there was a sharp blast from a trumpet.

The effect was immediate. Silence fell. Even the most drunken spectator lurched back to his seat and sat down quietly. All eyes were on the double doors of the guest-house. There was a murmur of excitement and anticipation.

The doors swung open. Moving slowly out into the bright lights of the arena came the Datin. She was seated on her throne, which was being carried by half a dozen of her 'attendants', including the judge and the young American pilot. She had replaced her earlier headdress with an even more elaborate one, and her eyes had been skilfully made up to give her an evil, cat-like leer. She truly was the Leopard Queen.

She was taken to the wooden platform and positioned opposite the crouching leopard. Her attendants ranged themselves around her. Dodi was amongst them. For the first time he was wearing full Kenyah costume.

The Datin stared slowly around the arena, fanning herself with a large ivory fan as she did so. She reminded the children of a strict teacher waiting for complete silence in class.

At last she seemed satisfied. Bending forwards slightly, she began to speak into a microphone that had been set up next to her throne. It was obviously some kind of welcoming speech, interrupted every so often by cheers and applause from the spectators. Hanna asked Jik what she was saying, but the Sea Gypsy boy was in no mood to translate. 'Some dam rubbish,' was all she could get out of him.

The speech ended, and the drums started up again.

The drummers were now in full view of the audience—half a dozen muscular, sweating men, pounding on banks of fat bamboo tomtoms, working themselves into a frenzy. Other men were positioning themselves at intervals around the edge of the arena. They were holding long steel-tipped spears. They stood with their legs apart, watching, waiting.

The Datin allowed her eyes to travel round the stadium once more. Then she called out a name.

A man stepped forward. It was the fat army general. Like the Datin's other attendants, he had shed his uniform and was wearing a loincloth and feathered headdress. With his big belly and short legs, he looked like a sumo wrestler. He was carrying a gleaming sword and an enormous, brightly painted shield, almost as big as himself.

He bowed to the Datin, climbed down from the platform, and went up to the crouching leopard. He put one foot on it, then turned and made a strange, yelping cry, which was immediately taken up by the crowd. The drums pounded in reply.

The moment had arrived.

There were shouts. A man was half-led, half-dragged down a caged walkway into the arena. He was naked apart from a loincloth. He was a Punan—the children could tell that by his pale skin and delicate features. As the spectators caught sight of him a great roar rose up. A sword and shield were thrust into his hands.

Half-blinded by the lights, the man hesitated,

staring apprehensively at the Datin; at the baying audience; and finally at his opponent. Then he peered down at the weapons he had been given. There was an appalled gasp from Ned. 'Have you seen his sword?'

It was made of wood—painted wood. It was like a child's toy—completely useless.

'And look at his goddam feet!' Jik exclaimed.

He was wearing leg irons. It was impossible for him to walk or run. There could be no escape.

32

Fight to the Death

The Punan was still staring hopelessly at his useless sword when the general attacked. He came in at a low, crouching run, swinging his sword like a scythe, threatening to sever the man's legs at the knees.

Escape seemed impossible, but the Punan thrust the point of his shield into the ground, and with perfect timing, used it to vault over the slashing blade.

The general's sword thudded into the soft wood of the shield and stuck fast. He tried desperately to wrench it free. As he did so, the Punan seized his chance and brought his wooden sword down with a loud thwack on the general's head.

Blood began to flow.

A huge cheer went up from the crowd. Despite their terror, Hanna and the boys found themselves joining in.

The general freed his sword with a jerk and backed away snarling. He was clearly not accustomed to being laughed at. He wiped the sweat and blood from his brow. 'Go get him!' Hanna heard Ned yell at the brave Punan. 'Go get him now!'

'Smack him in the goddam guts!' Jik screamed.

The boys almost sounded as if they were enjoying themselves.

The general tried a new tactic. He began to circle round his opponent, just out of reach, moving as fast as his stumpy legs could carry him, forcing the Punan to twist and turn to stay facing him. The general lunged; the Punan parried. Again and again he lunged. Each time his sword thudded uselessly against the Punan's shield.

Now the children understood: the general was trying to make his opponent dizzy. The moment that happened, with his legs chained together, he would surely fall over and the contest would be lost.

How much longer could he last?

The crowd was going wild, the drunken spectators screaming at the tops of their voices, hammering with their feet on the wooden staging. Suddenly Hanna knew what the scene reminded her of: Ancient Rome. It must have been like this— *exactly* like this—when the early Christians were forced out onto the blood-splattered floor of the Colosseum to face sword-wielding gladiators. There would have been the same braying banks of spectators; the same animal lust for blood. And in place of the Datin, with the absolute power of life and death, would have been the Emperor!

For a while the one-sided contest continued. Then the inevitable happened. The Punan slipped, the chains on his ankles tightened, and he pitched forwards, his sword and shield flying from his grasp.

His opponent was on to him in a flash, pinning him down with his foot, stabbing at his flesh with the point of his sword.

The children could see the defeated man's face clearly now, his cheeks distorting as he was pressed harder and harder into the dust. His eyes were closed. The fight was over. He was waiting to die. *'Bunuh!'* the crowd were screaming. *'Bunuh!'* *'KILL!'*

The general gripped the man's hair, jerked his head back. He glanced at the Datin. He was waiting for her signal.

For a long moment she remained motionless.

Then she brought her ivory fan down onto the arm of her throne with a sharp crack.

Hanna grabbed the boys and covered their eyes. There was no way she was going to let them see what happened next.

They didn't see, but they certainly heard.

There were three dull thuds. It sounded like

somebody chopping wood. Then the shout came—
a blood-curdling scream of triumph.

Hanna risked a glance through the window bars.

The fat general, his podgy body drenched in
blood and sweat, had climbed onto the crouching
leopard. In one hand he was clutching his sword,
in the other, the Punan's severed head. He was
holding them triumphantly aloft, obviously dedi-
cating them to the Leopard Queen.

'We've got to stop this!' Hanna exclaimed,
horrified. 'We've got to do something about it!'

'There's nothing we *can* do,' Ned replied in a
depressed voice.

He was right. They were completely helpless. All
they could do was wait until it was their turn to
die.

There was a short pause while the arena was
cleared, then the roars began again. Another 'contest' was under way. This time the swordsman was
the man the Datin had referred to as 'Your
Excellency'. She was clearly taking no risk that he
might be beaten. His opponent, who had to be virtually carried into the arena, was weak and sick—
hardly able to stand, let alone put up any sort of
fight.

The end came quickly, the killer blows—it took
six of them this time—thudding down as Hanna
and the boys once more hid their eyes.

The third contest involved the American pilot. This one took longer than the others—his opponent was clearly an experienced fighter—but the result, inevitably, was the same.

Fight followed fight, until Hanna stopped counting. She no longer made any attempt to see what was going on, but joined the boys back on the floor.

At Ned's suggestion they began to sing, in a desperate attempt to drown out the terrible sounds of death. The only songs they could think of were nursery rhymes: 'Twinkle Twinkle Little Star'; 'Old King Cole'; 'Here We Go Round The Mulberry Bush'. But even though they sang as loudly as they could, the sickening thud of the head-hunters' swords, and the brain-piercing screams of victory were still louder. How long before they themselves would be dragged out to their deaths, Hanna wondered, as the three children clung to each other for comfort.

They were halfway through 'Ba Ba Black Sheep' when the door of the Death House was suddenly wrenched open. Beckoning at them, his face flushed with excitement, was Dodi.

'Come!' he said. 'It is time!'

33

Jack the Giant Killer

It was a short walk across the floor of the arena to the foot of the Datin's throne, but to the children it seemed like a million miles. As the spectators caught sight of them a huge shout rose up. It was like a football crowd cheering its favourite players before an important match began. Hanna, Ned, and Jik were clearly the night's main attraction.

Hanna's reeling brain took in the scene. For the first time she understood what the decorated poles that had been set up earlier were for. More than half of them now bore a gruesome burden—a severed head.

She forced herself to look at each of them in turn. To her relief, Mini and Po were not amongst them. Where there was life there was hope, she told herself stupidly.

What hope?

In a very short while their own heads would be stuck up there. And so would Po's and Mini's. Let it be quick, she prayed. For God's sake let it be quick . . .

They halted in front of the throne. As Dodi resumed his seat behind her, the Datin spread her arms wide. 'Welcome to our *Begawai Mati*—our Festival of Death!' she exclaimed, her amplified voice bouncing off the sheer walls of Leopard Rock. 'I have already explained to the Brotherhood who you are, and what we are going to do with you. Believe me, they are as excited as I am. I have told them how very brave you all are, but I'm not sure they believe me. So we're going to find out! It's going to be a lot of fun for everybody—well, *almost* everybody.'

Hanna could control herself no longer. 'You're evil!' she screamed at the Datin. 'You're the most evil person on this planet!'

It was as if she'd cracked a joke—a very funny joke. Loud laughter broke out. 'I don't see what's so funny,' Hanna screamed.

'Nor do I!' Ned added, finally finding his voice.

The Datin smiled condescendingly. She turned to the crowd. 'You see what I mean? These children are as brave as lions—no, as brave as *leopards*!' She held up her hands with their sharpened, painted nails and made a clawing movement in their direction. 'Grrrr!'

Fresh laughter rose up.

'If you're going to kill us, just get it over with,'

Jik shouted furiously. 'Don't play goddam games with us!'

The Datin clapped her hands in glee. 'Even the Sea Gypsy boy is brave! I like you three kids so much! You remind me of myself when I was a girl. No, we're not going to kill you—at least not just yet. We've got something much more interesting lined up for you. You know the old fairy story— "Jack the Giant Killer"? It's going to be exactly like that—except there'll be three Jacks—you, Hanna, and Ned—and only one giant to kill! But what a giant! Guards! Bring on the prisoner!'

There was the sound of a struggle from somewhere behind the stage; the clank of chains; a deep bellow of rage. A buzz of excitement ran round the crowd. Everybody was staring at the caged walkway. Hanna, Ned, and Jik exchanged terrified glances.

A giant?

Surely there were no such creatures as giants?

It had to be another of the Datin's jokes . . .

The man who was finally thrust into the glare of the floodlights was enormous—nearly twice the height of the guards who were struggling with him—but to the children's relief he seemed to be human. He was clearly immensely strong. Even though he was wearing leg-irons, and his hands were pinioned behind his back, he managed to send two of his captors flying, and a third stumbled away clutching a bloody jaw.

'Stop that!'

The Datin's furious shout rang out into the night.

The prisoner paused, turned towards the stage. As he did so, the children were able to see his face for the first time.

It was Felix!

34

The Apparition

What on earth was going on? Were they looking at a *ghost*? Hanna, Ned, and Jik stared, open-mouthed, at the apparition before them.

Then Felix spotted them. He seemed even more shocked than they were. '*Gott im Himmel!*' he roared in German. 'God in Heaven! What are you three doing here? I thought you were in England.'

'We're looking for you!' Ned spluttered. 'No, not looking for you, looking for *clues*. You're supposed to be dead!'

'*Dead?*'

'Are you dam certain you are alive?' Jik asked fearfully.

'Do I look dead?' Felix exclaimed.

'No . . . but . . . '

Hanna rushed up to him. Grabbed his arm. He certainly *felt* real. 'They found a body,' she said frantically. 'They said it was you. Dad's been sentenced to death for your murder. He's going to be executed by firing squad in three—no, *two* days' time!'

'You joke.'

'She's not joking,' Ned thrust in. 'We were at the trial! We've been trying to prove he didn't do it so we can save him.'

Felix swung towards the Datin. 'This is your doing!' he bellowed furiously. 'It's got your vicious, evil name written all over it!'

The Datin gave a modest shrug, but said nothing. Fresh laughter rose from the crowd. It was like a sick comedy show—a pantomime of death.

Felix was right, Hanna realized. His 'murder' had been arranged by the Datin, just as she'd arranged everything else. She must have taken a headless corpse, planted his papers on it, and arranged for it to be 'discovered' floating in the river. No wonder it had been buried so quickly— even the simplest DNA test would have revealed the truth. Dad was then arrested—his bag of gold used as 'evidence'—and sentenced to death by the Datuk's brother, the judge. And all the time—all those days and weeks this was going on—Felix had been alive, locked away—no doubt in solitary confinement—here at Leopard Rock, ready for the children to arrive, as the Datin knew they surely would.

It was as if they were following a script, and tonight was the final act, the climax of months of careful planning. The timing was exquisite, and exquisitely cruel. For so long they'd been searching for evidence to prove that Dad was innocent, and finally they'd found it.

Not even the crookedest judge could allow somebody to be executed for murder when the victim was still alive!

Felix alone could save Dad.

Hanna knew it. The boys knew it.

So did the Datin.

Which was why they were going to be made to kill him.

It was the cleverest, most perfect act of revenge ever! At a stroke they would not only be murdering an innocent man, they would be destroying Dad's last and only chance of escaping the firing squad.

They would be killing their own father, as surely as they were killing his best friend.

The Datin had anticipated their thoughts. 'It's so neat!' she crowed. 'So very neat, don't you agree? And now it's giant-killing time! Please don't disappoint the Brotherhood. They've been waiting so long for this!'

Blind fury had overcome Ned's terror. 'Never!' he screamed at the Datin. 'You'll never make us kill anybody!'

A cruel smile played at the corners of her blood-red lips. 'Oh you're wrong there, Ned. So very wrong!'

She gestured with one of her scarlet-clawed hands. Felix was seized and dragged across to the crouching leopard. He was forced face-downwards onto it. The stained shirt he was wearing was ripped away, exposing his neck. It was to be his execution block, Hanna realized.

She was about to add her protests to Ned's when a sinewy arm wrapped itself round her neck, and a razor-sharp knife was pressed against her throat. As she struggled for breath, she saw that Jik had been seized by a second knifeman.

Only Ned remained free.

When he saw what had happened to Hanna and Jik, his defiance drained away. He looked like a scared rabbit caught in a car's headlights.

A guard approached him. He was carrying an exquisitely-engraved head-hunting sword. He placed it on the ground at Ned's feet, and went away.

Ned stared numbly at the sword.

'Pick it up!' the Datin ordered.

He made no move.

'I said pick it up! NOW!'

Ned shot a quick glance at Hanna and Jik. He was shaking his head as if denying to himself what was happening. After a moment's agonizing inde-cision, he slowly bent and picked up the weapon.

'That's better!' the Datin exclaimed. 'That's

much better! Now listen to me very carefully, Ned. You have a choice. A very simple choice. You can take your trusty sword and cut off the giant's head and *maybe* live happily ever after. Or you can do nothing and watch your sister and your best friend die slow, painful deaths. Which is it to be?'

As the Leopard Queen's amplified voice echoed away into the night, a profound hush fell. All eyes were on Ned. Silent tears were streaming down his face. 'I don't know what to do,' he said hopelessly, as if talking to himself. 'I don't know . . . '

'Come here.'

It was Felix who had spoken.

Ned went unsteadily across to him.

He stared calmly up at the terrified boy. 'You must kill me,' he said softly.

'I can't!' Ned gasped.

'Yes you can. You're brave enough, and strong enough. If you do it, there's just a chance they'll let you go. You are young and your whole life is before you. I am old, and am going to die anyway. Do not blame yourself for this. It is not your doing. Just make sure your aim is good, and hit me as hard as you can. Now I will say my prayers.'

His eyes closed, but his lips continued to move silently.

There was an excited shout from the crowd. It

turned instantly into an ear-splitting roar. Once more the Leopard Men were baying for blood.

'*Bunuh!*'

'*Bunuh!*'

'*KILL!*'

'*KILL!*'

Slowly, Ned raised the sword above his head. He was summoning up every bit of his strength, Hanna could tell, desperate to save Felix the agony of a second blow. Her heart went out to him. She loved her brother so much. So very much . . .

Then something quite unexpected happened.

The grip on her neck was suddenly loosened. The knife at her throat clattered to the ground. Her captor let out a loud groan and slumped down heavily at her feet.

At almost the same moment, the man holding Jik collapsed too.

Glancing at their twitching bodies, Hanna saw why.

Sticking out of their backs were half a dozen poisoned arrows.

35
Attack!

The last person Hanna saw before the floodlights went out, and all hell broke loose, was Ned. He was still standing next to Felix, with his sword raised. It was as if he'd been frozen stiff.

Charging past him into the arena, just visible in the pale moonlight, were dozens of lithe, bare-chested men. They were holding blowpipes, and had quivers of arrows slung from their waists. They were firing rapidly and accurately. The Leopard Men, most of whom were drunk, desperately tried to fight back, but were no match for their attackers. Headdresses askew, the Leopard Queen and her attendants leapt from the platform and dashed for safety into the guest-house.

'Hanna! Quick!'

It was Jik. Together they sprinted across to Ned. Hanna grabbed his sword and flung it away into the darkness. Then they bent to help Felix. Using the knife that had been held at his throat moments earlier, Jik swiftly cut the plastic straps that bound the big man's hands behind his back.

They helped him to his feet, but he could go nowhere. The chains on his ankles were too tight. 'Leave me!' Felix yelled, as a volley of shots narrowly missed them. 'Save yourselves while you've got the chance!'

Hanna was protesting that they'd *never* leave him when she spotted two familiar figures racing through the crowded arena towards them.

One was Mini, clutching a blowpipe, firing as she ran.

The other was Pak Mulut.

In one hand he held an automatic rifle; in the other, a pair of bolt cutters. With a swift movement he sliced through Felix's chains, freeing his legs. 'Follow me quick!' he yelled.

'Where are we going?' Hanna asked Mini, as Felix and the children dashed after him.

'Sangabera. To get your father free!'

'But how . . . ?'

'Stop asking questions! Just run!'

There were fights going on everywhere. Some of the Leopard Men were slashing out wildly with their head-hunting swords, but they were no match for the Punan's blowpipes and razor-sharp *parangs*. As they sprinted after the boatman, the children spotted a tall white man. He was using a blowpipe with deadly accuracy, picking off any opponent who looked dangerous.

It was Po. He stuck up a thumb as they sped past. 'Good luck!' he shouted above the din of battle. 'God be with you!'

'Isn't he coming with us?' Hanna yelled at Mini.

'No, he stays to help our people. My Po is the bravest man in the whole world!'

There was a sudden stutter of machine gun fire. It was coming from one of the watch-towers. A Punan fighter staggered back, clutching his arm, which was pouring with blood. 'I'll catch up with you!' Mini yelled.

Before they could stop her, she was gone, ducking and dodging between the fighters as she raced for the deep shadow beneath the tower. The machine-gunner didn't spot her. As his finger closed on the trigger to fire a second burst, Mini swung her blowpipe towards him.

He let out a sharp cry as her arrow pierced his flesh, injecting its deadly poison into his bloodstream. He pitched unconscious across the barrel of his gun. 'Got him!' yelled the little Punan girl gleefully as she raced back to rejoin the others.

There was a guard at the main entrance to the complex. He tried to stop them, but Pak Mulut silenced him with a burst of gunfire, and they were through.

They were heading for the quad bike. It was parked in the shadows at the side of the track.

Tossing his rifle to Felix, Pak Mulut jumped into the driving seat and the engine roared into life. Felix and the children swiftly jammed themselves into the tiny trailer. Lurching and bouncing on the rough track, the powerful machine accelerated through the night towards the river.

The stretch of jungle between Leopard Rock and the jetty, which had taken the children so long to cross on foot when they'd first arrived, took just a few minutes by quad bike going in the opposite direction. As they screeched to a halt next to the jetty, Pak Mulut's four sons were waiting in the *Maidah,* its engines running. Everybody scrambled on board and the mooring ropes were cast off.

36

The Chase

How could Mini possibly be right, Hanna wondered, as she flung herself down next to Ned. How could they possibly hope to get all the way to Sangabera in time to save Dad? There was no need to check the string in her pocket any more. There was just one day left now—just twenty-four hours—before the dreadful sentence would be carried out. It had taken them six—no, *seven*—days to come this far upstream. Only a plane could get them back in time.

She felt a rush of black despair. To be so close to success, and then to simply run out of days was so unfair! Ned was sitting silent and pale beside her. She took his hand. It would take weeks—*months* probably—for him to get over his terrifying ordeal in the arena. With Dad's death coming on top of that, he might never recover.

Then something extraordinary happened.

As they cleared the jetty, Pak Mulut's sons swung the longboat's nose downstream and pushed the throttles of the four huge Mercury engines to maximum.

It was like taking off in a drag car from a standing start. Thrust backwards by the violent acceleration, Felix and the children clung on for dear life as the boat began to rocket downriver through the darkness. It was impossible to say how fast they were going—sixty, seventy—maybe even eighty miles an hour! The brute power that had propelled them upstream day after day against the raging current, was now working *with* the river instead of against it.

Pak Mulut was crouched in the bow, holding a powerful spotlight. He kept it trained on the raging waters ahead, signalling frantically as he identified lethal rocks and rapids. One mistake, Hanna knew, and they would be instantly smashed to pieces.

As the forest flashed past, her despair gradually changed to hope. If they could maintain this speed anything was possible!

After an hour or so, Pak Mulut allowed himself to relax a little. There were no more rapids for a while. Hanna grabbed the chance to go forward to talk to him. Were they really going to make it to Sangabera in time?

He shrugged. 'Maybe. If the chasing people don't catch us.'

'What chasing people?' she asked, horrified.

He pointed back upstream. In the far

distance a light could just be seen, winking and gleaming between the jungle trees. 'They got a boat from somewhere,' he said matter-of-factly. 'But we got good engines—the best. They won't catch us. Unless . . . '

'Unless what?'

'Unless we hit a rock. Unless our engines break. Unless we got no more fuel.'

'But there's plenty of fuel!' Hanna protested, remembering the big plastic drums at the back of the boat.

'Not enough for Sangabera. We got to get more. But to get it we got to stop, and then the chasing people catch up with us.'

Her anxiety increased. 'Who are these chasing people?'

'Who knows? Dodi maybe. Other pigs like him. I should have killed them all when I got the chance!'

'But I thought Dodi was your friend.'

Pak Mulut snorted. 'Him? I spit on him!' As if to prove it, he shot a big gobbet of phlegm into the river.

'Why are you helping us?' a deep voice cut in. 'Why are you risking your life for us?'

It was Felix. He'd come forward to join them.

The boatman's eyes narrowed. 'To get my revenge,' he hissed.

'Revenge for what?'

'For what they do to my tribe. I am a Kenyah. This Brotherhood—these stinking Leopard Men— they say they are Kenyah, but they are not. They steal everything from us—our dances, our legends, our songs—and make them dirty with their blood-letting. They are murderers, vicious murderers, and worst of all is their queen. So I say to myself, Pak Mulut, you must stop all this. You must take your revenge.

'I am a contractor. I build houses for these animals. They trust me. Every week I bring building materials upriver. I bring drainage pipes. Inside the drainage pipes I put blowpipes, poison arrows, *parangs*. I can bring only a few each time, but after many weeks there are enough. Then it is easy. While everybody watches the head-taking, I cut a hole in the cage of the Punan. I hand them the weapons. The rest you have seen with your own eyes.'

'You've saved all our lives!' Felix exclaimed.

The boatman shrugged. 'I am pleased for that, but your lives mean little compared to my revenge. And now I must look to the river. There are many dangerous rapids ahead.'

He turned away. The conversation was over.

Dawn began to break, its greeny-grey light filtering through the branches of the riverside trees.

Only now did Hanna fully appreciate just how fast they were going. With the wind ripping at her hair, and spray stinging her cheeks, she felt as if she was flying. There were waterfalls up ahead—a whole chain of them—but Pak Mulut gave no signal to slow down. Instead he threw the *Maidah* at them, at times twisting the bow through a hundred and eighty degrees as the current turned back on itself. 'We're coming to get you, Dad!' Hanna screamed, exhilarated.

Her eyes met Ned's. His blank expression had gone, and there was a hint—just a hint—of a smile on his lips.

She glanced back upriver. With the coming of the day, the light from the chasing boat had faded and disappeared. It was now impossible to tell just how far behind them it was—or even if it was still there. With any luck it had hit a rock and sunk without trace.

Bottled water was handed round. Jik took some to Pak Mulut and sat next to him as he drank it. He clearly hero-worshipped the taciturn boatman, and was asking him question after question about the boat and the river. To Hanna's surprise, Pak Mulut seemed quite happy to provide the answers.

Felix fell asleep, exhausted by the night's events. But for Hanna sleep was impossible. A thought was nagging at her. Had they really got a full day left before Dad's execution took place?

Mini was able to put her mind at rest. She'd asked Po exactly that question, and he'd told her that executions in Sangabera were always carried out on the stroke of midnight.

There was still time!

'We will be triumphant,' the little Punan girl announced. 'I can feel it in my skin.'

'You mean in your bones,' Hanna corrected.

'In my skin *and* my bones!'

She flashed Ned an affectionate smile, which was returned.

The rapids were eventually left behind, and as the morning wore on, the first signs of human occupation came into view on the valley sides—patches of forest felled to provide clearings for hill rice. Harvest was over now, and the spindly thatched huts, which the reapers had occupied when they kept watch over their crops, were deserted. Here and there blue smoke spiralled upwards as fresh areas of ground were burned to clear them for next season's planting.

They reached the logging camps. Large rafts of felled jungle trees, lashed together with ropes, were awaiting their long journey downstream.

As they approached the first of the rafts, which was almost as wide as the river, there was a frantic shout from Karmin, Pak Mulut's eldest son. One of the *Maidah*'s four engines had stopped.

A second engine spluttered into silence soon afterwards.

They were out of fuel!

Glancing back Hanna saw that the semi-transparent drums of gasoline powering the remaining two engines were almost empty too. The race to Sangabera had come to a sudden and catastrophic halt.

Pak Mulut didn't seem worried. He gave a quick signal. His sons brought the boat slowly alongside the log raft and tied up to it.

'What are you doing?' Hanna asked, alarmed.

'We wait,' the boatman replied.

'But we can't wait! My father is . . . '

He ignored her. Grabbing a *parang* he jumped onto the bobbing raft. His four sons joined him. They too had *parangs*. They began to carefully chop at the bindings that connected the outermost tree trunks to the rest. They worked swiftly and methodically, leaving just a handful of ropes uncut. Then they returned to the boat. Pak Mulut settled himself once more in the bow. His sons returned to the stern, where they transferred what remained of the gasoline into one of the empty drums. When they'd finished, it was less than a quarter full, but it was enough to power a single engine quite a long way if it was driven slowly. They connected it up, pressed the starter. The engine rumbled into life, but they made no attempt to cast off.

What on earth was happening? Felix, who'd woken up when they'd stopped, was as alarmed as the children. 'Shouldn't we get going?' he asked urgently.

Pak Mulut shook his head. 'Have patience.'

Hanna exploded. 'But we can't just—'

She didn't finish. The roar of high-powered engines shattered the silence of the river valley. A sharp-nosed longboat, painted bright red, curved into sight round a bend. It was travelling at high speed. Seated in its bow, clutching an automatic rifle, was Dodi.

Pak Mulut thrust his gun into Felix's hands. 'If he shoots, shoot back!' he ordered. 'You kids get down!'

The children did what they were told. As she pressed herself to the oil-stained floorboards, Hanna's new-found optimism vanished. With only one working engine, and hardly any fuel, how could the *Maidah* possibly hope to escape?

They were sitting ducks!

There was a burst of automatic fire. Bullets drilled through the side of the boat immediately above her head. An answering burst from Felix produced a shout of pain from their pursuers. The big man was obviously a good shot.

Still Pak Mulut waited. Surely they should at least *try* to get away! Did he want to commit suicide?

There was more gunfire—but this time it was wide and high. Braving the bullets, Hanna raised her head and peered out. Their pursuers were less than two hundred metres away, closing in rapidly. Felix was crouched in the *Maidah's* stern, firing steadily back at them. Most of his shots splashed harmlessly into the river, but he was succeeding brilliantly in putting Dodi off his aim.

The red boat was a hundred metres away now.

Fifty . . .

At the very last moment, Pak Mulut and his sons sprang into action. In a precise, co-ordinated movement, they reached over the side and swung their *parangs* at the remaining ropes that held the log raft together.

They parted with a loud twang.

The effect was instantaneous. Gripped by the racing current, the outer tree trunks broke away from the rest and swung violently across the river.

There was no way of avoiding them. As the *Maidah* fled downstream on its one remaining engine, their pursuers slammed into the logs at high speed.

They acted like a launching ramp. Its engines screaming, the boat shot skywards in a graceful arc, before nose-diving onto the disintegrating raft and bursting into a massive ball of flame.

37
Terror from Above

Felix and the children stared at the burning boat, open-mouthed with astonishment. Had Pak Mulut *known* what was going to happen? It was impossible for anybody to have survived a crash like that. Dodi was surely dead. But what about the Datin? Had she been on board the boat too?

Mini asked Pak Mulut. He shrugged. 'Maybe. Maybe not.' He was peering at the river once more, searching for the swiftest currents to help their protesting single engine along. It was as if the spectacular events of a few moments earlier had never happened.

After an hour of frustratingly slow progress, the *Maidah* pulled alongside a small floating jetty. Next to it was Pak Mulut's fuel dump. Swiftly, full drums of gasoline were wheeled on board and connected up. Within minutes all four engines were once more giving out their familiar, throaty roar. 'Now we get going properly!' the boat owner annnounced. It was the first time he'd shown any sign of excitement. He slipped a digital watch from his wrist and handed it to Ned. 'You are the time-keeper,' he told him with a smile.

Hanna glanced at the watch as her brother strapped it on. To her dismay she saw that it was already two p.m. There were just ten hours left before midnight. Even with their engines back to full power, could they really get to Sangabera in time to save Dad?

The Kerai was wider now, silt-brown, the giant forest trees which had lined its banks long gone. There were other boats on the river, mostly small motorized canoes. Their occupants' heads swivelled in alarm as the *Maidah* thundered past.

Long Gia hurtled into view. It was market day, and its jetty was crowded with small boats selling fruit and vegetables. There were furious shouts as the metre-high wave thrown up by the *Maidah*'s wash threatened to swamp them all. His eyes glued to the river ahead, Pak Mulut didn't spare them a second glance.

For hour after hour they raced southwards, past rice fields and ramshackle villages. Painted Kenyah tombs lined the far bank, bringing back uncomfortable memories of the horrific Death House. A pair of black eagles soared like avenging spirits above them.

Hanna glanced at Mini. The girl's usually

cheerful face was tight with worry. 'What's wrong?' she asked.

'I am fearful for my Po,' came the almost inaudible answer.

In their headlong race to save Dad, it was easy to forget that Mini's guardian had been left facing deadly danger too. 'I'm sure he'll be all right,' Hanna told her. 'He's very brave.'

Mini nodded. 'Oh, he's brave! He's the bravest man in the whole world! But I think he's *too* brave. I think he takes too many chances. I want him to save himself, not just everybody else. What will I do if any harm befalls him?'

'You could come and live with us,' Ned suggested, overhearing the conversation and trying to be helpful.

Mini shook her head violently. 'I don't *want* to come and live with you! I don't want to live in England where it's cold and rainy. I want to stay here, in the forest, with my Po and my Uncle Irang and my Auntie Tama. Oh, why do these terrible things have to happen? Why can't we all just live in peace?'

'Because of evil, greedy people like the Datin,' Jik put in bitterly. 'That's why people have to dam fight. I hope she's dead and has gone to hell!'

While they'd been talking, the *Maidah* had rounded a broad bend. Ahead of them was a long,

290

deserted stretch of river. With no obstructions to worry about, the battered longboat seemed to draw in a deep breath and hurl itself forward with fresh vigour. Hanna gripped its sides tightly, willing it onwards, faster and faster.

She felt a sharp nudge in her ribs. It was Ned. He was pointing upwards. High above them was a plane.

It was dull green, and its shape was sickeningly familiar.

As they watched, its nose dipped and it dived down towards them, gathering speed as it did so.

In the brief instant before it passed overhead, Hanna got a clear view through its cockpit window.

At the controls was the young American pilot.

Seated beside him was the Datin, her face distorted with fury and hatred.

The aircraft swept upriver, then banked steeply to make a second pass. As it did so, a side window opened, and a bejewelled, red-clawed hand was thrust out. It was holding a machine-pistol.

The children screamed out a warning, but Pak Mulut had already seen the gun. He signalled briskly to his sons.

Instantly the *Maidah* began to change course, zigzagging crazily from bank to bank. A line of bullets zipped across the water, missing them by centimetres. Felix grabbed his rifle and began to fire back. But after three or four shots, there was a loud click. Its magazine was empty. He threw down the weapon in disgust.

They were helpless.

Or were they?

As the plane turned to renew its attack, Pak Mulut gestured sharply at Hanna. He was pointing at a small locker close to where she was sitting. Reaching quickly into it she found a cheap make-up bag. It had the name Maidah scrawled across it. It obviously belonged to the boat owner's wife.

She ripped it open. It was full of half-used lipsticks and mascaras. At the bottom of the bag was a pink-framed hand-mirror, identical to the one the mad woman had used to admire herself on that weird night back at Pak Mulut's house in Long Gia.

Hanna stared at the bag, puzzled. What good was a load of cheap make-up against an attacking aircraft?

Then the penny dropped.

She gave Pak Mulut a quick thumbs-up to show she'd understood, then tipped the contents of the bag onto the floor. She grabbed the mirror and polished it swiftly on her shirt.

The American pilot must have spotted Felix throwing down his gun, because his next run was slower, and more deliberate. The aircraft came in low—very low—just a few metres above the surface of the water. At the last minute the *Maidah* stopped zigzagging and levelled out to face it. Bullets began to spray from the Datin's gun, but Hanna ignored them.

She knew exactly what she had to do.

Fighting to control her shaking hands, she pointed the mirror at the brilliant tropical sun, then angled it at the approaching plane.

Her aim was good. A dazzling beam of reflected light shot straight into the pilot's eyes.

Blinded, he instinctively threw up an arm to shade himself. As he did so, the aircraft dipped sideways.

It was a fatal error.

He was flying too low. There was no room to recover.

Hanna caught a glimpse of the Datin's terrified face, as the plane's left wing-tip hit the brown, swirling water in the *Maidah*'s wake.

It cartwheeled twice, sending up a huge plume of spray, then broke in half and sank without trace.

No, not *quite* without trace.

For a brief instant a bejewelled, red-clawed hand could be seen waving above the surface, the machine-pistol it was holding still pumping bullets skywards.

38

Race to the Finish

It was as if Hanna had scored a goal in an important football match. Jik, Mini, and Ned were cheering wildly. Felix was slapping her on the back. Even Pak Mulut's stony face had broken into a smile.

She didn't join in their celebration. Shouldn't they try to rescue the Datin and the pilot, she asked anxiously, stunned by what she'd just done. The boatman shook his head. The current was too strong, he told her. The river too deep. There would be no survivors.

It was over.

The most evil woman in Borneo—in the whole world, probably—was dead. The Leopard Queen had finally been cheated of her revenge!

But had she?

Even from beyond the grave, she would still triumph if they couldn't get to Sangabera in time to save Dad.

Now it really was a race to the finish.

With Pak Mulut directing their course, the *Maidah* found yet more speed from somewhere, and rocketed onwards. There was still such a long way to go!

Using the boatman's watch, Ned began to count down the time.

Now there were eight hours left before midnight.

Now seven.

Now six . . .

Far ahead of them a plume of smoky haze marked the location of the capital of East Borneo, and the prison where Dad was facing his last evening on earth. If only they could contact the governor so the execution could be delayed until they got there! But there were no phone masts this far upriver, and no number to call even if there had been. Hanna tried telepathy—sending a message using the power of thought alone—but gave up. She knew it wouldn't work, and it just made her feel stupid.

Now just five hours remained.

Night fell. Pak Mulut was once more crouched in the bows scanning the swirling surface of the river with his spotlight, searching for floating logs or other obstructions that could sink the *Maidah* in an instant.

Felix handed round packets of food that the crew gave him—more cold rice and pork wrapped in banana leaves. It was greasy and tasteless, but at least it was food.

He joined the children while they ate, perching next to Ned on one of the benches. 'How's it going?' he asked, as they peeled open their packets of rice.

'Fine,' Ned replied.

'You don't sound fine to me,' the big man commented.

'That's because I'm not!' Ned suddenly burst out. 'Felix, I wouldn't have cut your head off! I really wouldn't have!'

His voice was choked with anguish.

For a moment or two there was silence. Then Felix looped an arm round the trembling boy and gave him an affectionate hug. 'If I'd thought you would have done I'd have thrown you overboard long ago,' he said cheerfully. 'So why don't we forget about it and never talk about it again?'

Ned looked up at him, tears of relief glistening in his eyes. 'You mean that?'

'Of course I mean it.'

'Cool!' said Jik, sounding as relieved as his best friend. 'Isn't that goddam cool? Mini?'

'Das ist wunderbar!' commented the little Punan girl in perfect German, a language that Hanna had no idea she knew.

Now there were four hours left . . .

Now just three . . .

The talking was over. There was nothing left to

say or do except wait and hope. They sat in silence as the *Maidah* raced onwards. Sangabera was clearly visible now: its glimmering rows of street-lights interspersed with the glow of neon shop-signs and the flash of car headlights as traffic lurched through its potholed streets.

So close, and yet still so far away . . .

Two hours . . .

Surging beneath bridges, dodging moored freighters and coal barges, the *Maidah* thundered into Sangabera docks. Ahead of them was a ram-shackle warehouse with part of its roof missing.

Slackening their speed only in the last few seconds, Pak Mulut's four sons swung the boat skilfully to a halt alongside it.

One hour . . .

'Out!' yelled the boatman, pointing at a battered jeep parked near the warehouse.

He sprinted across to it, followed by Felix and the children. With Felix in the passenger seat, and Hanna, Ned, Jik, and Mini clinging on desperately in the back, he gunned its engine into life, and squealed up a narrow exit road onto the highway.

'How far is the prison?' Hanna yelled.

'Too far!' Pak Mulut yelled back.

What followed was the craziest, most terrifying drive of the children's life. Racing down main roads and back-alleys, dodging red lights and protesting traffic policemen, scattering chairs and tables and diners in open-air restaurants; sometimes on four wheels, sometimes on two, the ancient jeep screamed towards the distant suburb where the prison was situated.

Thirty minutes . . .

The forbidding steel-spiked walls of the prison loomed out of the night. Its main gates were to the south. Pak Mulut swerved the jeep towards them.

Hanna had expected the place to be deserted when they got there.

She was wrong.

The prison forecourt was heaving with people. There were reporters everywhere, jabbering urgently into microphones. There were lights. Camera crews. Grouped to one side were demonstrators holding placards protesting against capital punishment. Dad's execution was clearly world news.

The jeep screamed to a halt beside a cluster of camera vans, and Felix leapt out. He powered his way past cables and lights and placards towards the prison gates, thrusting people aside as he went. Hanna, Ned, Jik, and Mini chased desperately in his wake.

'It's the missing kids!' somebody shouted in English, recognizing them.

The cry was taken up. 'It's the kids!'

Reporters surged towards them, microphones outstretched, but the children dodged them, ducking and weaving through a forest of legs. Felix was hammering on the gates with both fists when they caught up with him. 'Open up right now!' he was roaring in a mixture of English and Indonesian. 'Nick Bailey's innocent! Stop this execution!'

A reporter had recognized Felix too. 'That's the bloke Bailey was supposed to have murdered!' he yelled. 'He's still alive!'

The protesters took up the shout. *'Nick Bailey's innocent! Nick Bailey's innocent! FREE HIM! FREE HIM!'*

Security cameras mounted on the prison wall swivelled, and zoomed in on Felix and the children. But still the gates remained stubbornly closed.

Fifteen minutes . . .

Ten minutes . . .

'FREE NICK BAILEY! FREE NICK BAILEY!' It was no longer a chant, but a roar, taken up by protesters and newsmen alike.

Would nobody inside listen? Would nobody open the gates and let them in?

Five minutes . . .

Four minutes . . .

Suddenly the gates swung open. Felix and the children were quickly ushered through.

Mum was waiting for them in a small court-yard, her face pale and drawn.

With her was Miss Wiyati the lawyer, and Mr Bennett from the British Embassy.

Hurrying towards them was a small bald-headed man the children hadn't seen before. He was the prison governor. He went up to Felix and stared intently at his face, glancing down at a pic-ture he was holding, obviously comparing the two. He looked highly agitated.

'Don't worry, I'm not a fake!' the big man growled.

'This is very irregular,' the governor said in heavily-accented English. 'I do not think I have the power to stop this thing . . . '

'Oh yes you do!' roared Felix, who looked as if he might grab the little man and throttle him with his bare hands. 'Stop it now!'

Three minutes . . .

Two minutes . . .

'There'll be serious political repercussions,' Mr Bennett from the embassy said smoothly. 'You per-sonally will be blamed. I wouldn't like to be in your shoes when the President hears of this.'

The governor was sweating heavily.

One minute . . .

No minutes . . .

The children closed their eyes, waiting for the volley of shots that would tear their lives apart for ever.

It never came.

The governor had taken a hand-held radio from a holder on his belt and was barking orders into it, gesticulating wildly as he did so.

Soon afterwards, Dad was escorted into the yard. His hands were still tied; his eyes blindfolded. The blindfold was taken off him and he peered around.

'You took your time!' he said to Felix and the children.

Then he collapsed into Mum's arms and burst into tears.

TWO WEEKS LATER

39

Coming Home

The twin-engined Islander BN2B taxied across the concrete apron of Sangabera airport, reached the end of the runway, turned and began its take-off run. On board, as it lifted off over the open-cast coal mines and oil palm plantations that ringed the city, were seven passengers—Mum, Dad, Felix, Hanna, Ned, Jik, and Mini. Ned, who was still recovering from his ordeal at Leopard Rock, had been allowed to sit in the co-pilot's seat as a special favour by the friendly Australian pilot.

It was such a relief to get out of the sweltering, smelly capital city. Since that terrible night at the prison, the whole family—Felix included— had been caught up in a seemingly endless round of debriefings and media interviews. It was the biggest scandal to hit the province in decades.

Following an initial report to the provincial governor, an elite squad of commandos had been sent to Leopard Rock, prepared to take the place by force if necessary. There had been no need. When they arrived they'd been faced by an extraordinary sight.

Chained together by the ankles, hard at work in the rice fields under the hot tropical sun, was a motley collection of well-known public figures. In addition to Dad's trial judge, there were politicians and industrialists, financiers and senior army officers—even a famous professional footballer. Overseeing them, blowpipes at the ready, was a group of nomadic Punan tribesmen, led by an extraordinary Englishman called James Erskine.

A TV crew had captured the whole thing on film. Watching it in their Sangabera hotel room, Mini had let out a scream of pure joy when a familiar figure appeared on the screen. 'It's Po! He's alive! He's well!'

Her happiness knew no bounds when an interviewer spoke to him. 'Before I say anything,' Po began, 'I've got a message for a certain little girl, the bravest person I know. Well done, Mini—and come home soon, I miss you!'

'I'm coming home!' she told the TV screen, as if Po could hear her from where she was. She swung to the others. 'I'm going home and you're not stopping me!'

'We're not going to stop you,' Dad said with a big grin. 'In fact we're coming with you. Felix and I have just decided that.'

'And me,' said Mum.

'And us,' chorused Hanna, Ned, and Jik.

The plane was provided by the government, and after yet another lengthy debriefing session, when they were informed that the rest of the surviving Leopard Men had been discovered securely locked in the holding cage next to the arena, and were being brought downriver to face trial at Sangabera along with the VIPs, they were given permission to go.

The flight was spectacular, following the now-familiar course of the mighty Kerai River. At Felix's request, they took a diversion to Leopard Rock.

It looked the same as ever: brooding and mysterious. As they circled it, the children excitedly pointed out familiar landmarks: the overhang where they'd spent their uncomfortable twenty-four hours before being captured; the track to the jetty; the guest house and barracks; and, of course, the dreadful, blood-soaked arena. There were armed commandos stationed outside the Death House, which was sealed with yellow scene-of-crime tapes. After investigations were complete, the entire complex would be demolished, the pilot told them, and the area round the Rock returned to virgin jungle. Ned, who had been secretly dreading seeing the place again, clapped his hands in glee. Jik joined in his celebrations.

Three quarters of an hour later, the plane dipped down through a blanket of rainforest cloud. Beneath them was a jungle airstrip. With immense skill, the pilot brought the Islander down to a smooth landing, and its engine cut.

Hurrying towards them was a crowd of familiar people. Striding in the lead was a tall, thin white man. Even before the propellers had stopped turning, the door was wrenched open and a small figure flung herself horizontally out of the plane, into his arms. *'Akeu molé!'* Mini was screaming, covering his face with kisses. 'I have come home!'

Uncle Irang and Auntie Tama arrived next, followed by the rest of the villagers. Bringing up the rear was Asik the old blowpipe maker, who'd given them his canoe, and Lawai, his jolly wife. With them were Bahu and Leko, wagging their tails excitedly.

There were hugs and kisses all round. When she finally turned back to the others, Mini's face was alight with happiness. 'There's going to be a big *ramai* tonight,' she said. 'A big celebration. There's going to be dancing and singing and lots and lots of food to eat—the men have killed two fat pigs and one large deer. We're going to have such fun!'

As darkness fell, flares were lit all round the village, and after everybody had eaten their fill, the

dancing began. The music came from *sampehs*—
guitar-like instruments that produced a strange,
haunting rhythm.

The Punan dances were gentle, and rather sad.
Mini explained that it was because so many innocent Punan people had died, and it was difficult to
be cheerful.

But then, suddenly, the mood changed.
Somebody produced a bamboo drum, other
people took out nose-flutes, and the rhythm picked
up speed.

Out of the darkness leapt five Kenyah warriors.
They were carrying swords and shields, and wearing hornbill feather headdresses.

For one sickening moment Hanna thought it
was the Leopard Men come to avenge their defeat.
Ned looked ready to run for his life.

But then firelight lit up the newcomers' faces.

It was Pak Mulut and his four sons!

They were expert dancers, far better than any of
the so-called Brotherhood, and as they whirled
and twisted and stamped their feet, their pride
and pleasure in what they were doing shone
through. For the first time Hanna truly understood
what a profound and unforgivable insult it must
have been to have had their ancient tribal customs
hijacked by a group of murderous upstarts.

After a while the swords were put away for

safety's sake and everybody joined in the dancing, young and old—even Asik and Lawai. The old lady had taken a particular shine to Felix, and insisted on being whisked round the dance floor in his arms. A tame hornbill watched intently from a nearby rooftop, making loud *kwark* noises that were *almost* in time with the music.

Pak Mulut disappeared and returned soon afterwards with several plastic bottles full of *arak*. Now the party had really started!

When the children finally staggered off to bed in Po's house, the drinking and dancing was still going on, and continued far into the tropical night.

They made a late start the following morning. Many of the men—including Dad, Felix, and Po—had bad hangovers, which Mum said they thoroughly deserved. Carrying food and water for the day, everybody made their way down to the river where the *Maidah* was moored. The bullet-holes in the boat's wooden side had been sealed with temporary patches, which gave it the look of a wounded warrior.

Hanna, Ned, Jik, Mum, Dad, Felix, Mini, and Po clambered on board, along with most of the population of the village. There were only a few centimetres of dry planking left above the water-line. The four great engines started up, and Pak Mulut directed the laden boat slowly upstream.

They were heading for a small tributary with a familiar name—*Ba Daha*—Blood River. After a while they had to abandon the *Maidah,* because the water had become too shallow, and continue on foot.

When they finally reached Blood River Hanna gave a gasp of surprise. A squad of Punan villagers had travelled there a few days earlier and removed all trace of the gold workings. The valley had been returned to its original state, the river flowing swiftly and freely again.

They picnicked in the shade of a spreading forest tree, and then, when everybody was ready, they assembled next to the water. Uncle Irang made a long speech in the Punan language. He was talking to the river, Mini explained, asking its forgiveness for everything that had happened.

When he had finished, Dad and Felix stepped forward. They were each holding a small black bag. They were silent for a moment, staring down at the swirling stream, then they opened their bags and emptied the contents into the water.

For a brief instant there was a flash of gold.

And then it was gone.

David Miller was born in Norfolk. He has worked in advertising for most of his career, as a copy-writer, and later as a creative director.

He has travelled widely all over the world, and lived and worked in Malaysia and Singapore for more than ten years. *Leopard's Claw* is his third book in the best-selling Shark Island series. To research it, David travelled by boat and on foot into the remote rainforests of central Borneo.

David now writes full-time, and lives in Hampshire with his wife Su' en and his daughter Hanna.